Eager Star

★★★★★

Winnie

The Horse Gentler

2

TYNDALE KIDS

Tyndale House Publishers, Inc.
Carol Stream, Illinois

Eager Star

DANDI DALEY MACKALL

Visit Tyndale's exciting Web site for kids at www.tyndale.com/kids and the Winnie the Horse Gentler Web site at www.winniethehorsegentler.com.

You can contact Dandi Daley Mackall through her Web site at www.dandibooks.com.

Tyndale Kids logo is a trademark of Tyndale House Publishers, Inc.

Eager Star

Designed by Jacqueline L. Nuñez

Edited by Ramona Cramer Tucker

Scripture quotations are taken from the *Holy Bible*, New Living Translation, copyright © 1996. Used by permission of Tyndale House Publishers, Inc., Carol Stream, Illinois 60188. All rights reserved.

For manufacturing information regarding this product, please call 1-800-323-9400.

ISBN 978-0-8423-5543-8, mass paper

Printed in the United States of America

16   15
17   16   15   14

For Katy Mackall,
my terrific daughter.
I couldn't do these
books without you.
Thanks!

Chapter 1

*W*innie, stop her! She'll hurt Towaco!" Hawk shouted at me as she fumbled with the gate.

Nickers, my white Arabian, reared, pawing the air, daring Victoria Hawkins's Appaloosa to set foot on *her* turf, the paddock behind our barn. Towaco hung his head and tucked his tail to his haunches.

"It's okay, Hawk," I said, trying to sound calm. But watching my powerful Arabian threaten Hawk's little Appaloosa made me feel anything but calm. I was supposed to be Winnie the Horse Gentler, not Winnie the Horse Referee.

I picked a handful of grass and vaulted over the fence just as Nickers stretched her long, muscular neck and charged poor Towaco. The Appy whinnied. Hawk screamed.

"Nickers, come!" I called.

Towaco huddled close to the barn.

It had been only five minutes since Hawk's mom dropped off the Appaloosa. It had taken Hawk a few weeks to convince her mother to leave Towaco in my care. Watching that trailer bounce up our road was the proudest moment of my life because inside rode my first customer. Hawk had chosen to move her horse out of the fancy, high-priced Stable-Mart and into my little barn because she believed I could help Towaco. Her horse would be the first of many problem horses I could gentle. I wished Mom had been alive to see it.

But my pride had evaporated fast, like water in this sweltering Ohio heat. The second I turned our guest horse into the paddock, Nickers, my sweet Arabian, had wheeled around and kicked, missing the frightened Appy by inches.

"Nickers?" I called, willing a friendly tone and holding out my handful of grass.

She came but only after craning her neck around so Towaco could get a good look at her beautiful white teeth and her angry ears, flattened back in a horse threat. Then, for good measure, Nickers kicked out one hind leg, like a playful colt.

Towaco squealed as if Nickers had connected with her kick.

"Winnie!" Hawk yelled, as if I'd kicked her horse myself.

Nickers trotted up and nuzzled my outstretched palm, taking the scraggly grass I offered. I scratched behind her ears. "That's a good girl," I said, soothing her.

"Good girl?" Hawk's voice trembled.

I turned to look at her. Victoria Hawkins comes from Native American ancestry. She's tall and beautiful, with sleek black hair that falls straight to her waist. Unlike me—I'm short, with long, dark hair that has a mind of its own, a voice that sounds hoarse, and freckles that make people call me cute. I hate *cute*.

Usually Hawk's calm, Quarter Horse temperament makes me look like a wild Mustang. Not today. Her cheeks flushed as red as the pet bird on her shoulder, mimicking, *"Squawk! Good girl?"*

"Not *good*. That horse is still a Wild Thing!" Hawk insisted.

That's what people used to call my horse. But when she had become mine, I'd named her

Nickers. Nickers *is* good. She's great. And I love her so much it hurts. Getting to own my white Arabian had been more than a dream come true. It had taken a miracle. Now it was beginning to look like keeping her would take another.

My plan to pay for her upkeep was to gentle horses. People would pay me to fix their problem horses. But so far nobody knew about me. Gaining a reputation isn't easy when you're 12. But for 10 of my 12 years I lived with the best horse trainer in the world—my mom. Back in Wyoming people had come from miles around just to watch Mom talk wild horses into gentle companions.

But then Mom died in a horrible car accident, and everything changed. Dad, Lizzy, and I tried living in the *I* states—Illinois, Indiana, and Iowa—before landing in Ohio. We rented the last house in Ashland—right on the outskirts of the city limits, although Ashland's no city. The barn and pasture came with the house. We'd been here two months, and Dad had decided we'd stick with Ashland for the whole school year. But so far, except for Towaco, no problem horses had shown up. I'd tried posters, e-mail

bulletin boards, and even an ad in the paper.
I needed a reputation, and I needed it fast.

"Hawk," I said, scratching the crest of Nickers'
mane to keep her with me. "Horses go through
power struggles. Nickers figures she's the boss
since she was here first. Don't worry."

Hawk glared at Nickers. "I do not like it." Her
words came out separated, each one hard as ice.
If Hawk were a horse, she'd be an Andalusian, a
noble breed from Spain. Andalusians are classy,
strikingly beautiful, but you can't be too sure
where you stand with them. I thought Hawk
and I had a pretty good friendship going, but
she still acted different around her old friends. I
wondered how it would all work when school
started.

I glanced toward the house and spotted Lizzy,
my younger sister, halfway up the oak tree.
"Hawk, why don't you hang out with Lizzy. I'll
ride some of the orneriness out of Nickers. By
the time we get back, she'll be good. Okay?"

"Okay! Okay!" squawked Hawk's chattering
lory, named Peter, after an old actor Peter Lorre,
who used to play in scary or gangster movies.

"Maybe Peter and I should stay with
Towaco." Hawk reached over the gate, trying to

get her horse to come. But Towaco wouldn't budge from his safe spot by the barn.

"One hour, Hawk," I reasoned. "Let him get used to the pasture on his own."

Hawk stared at the pasture as if it were booby-trapped. Finally she said, "One hour."

As soon as Hawk left, I dashed to the barn for the hackamore, a bitless bridle I'd been using with Nickers, who resented the bit. In seconds I'd slipped on the leather hackamore and adjusted the rawhide loop that fits like a halter around Nickers' muzzle and behind her ears. As I led Nickers out of the pasture, she nuzzled the back of my neck and nickered with a low, rattling sound that never fails to melt my heart.

"I know, Nickers," I said, swinging up on her bareback. "You didn't mean any harm. But you have to be nice to Towaco. We need Hawk's money to buy your oats. And I need the reputation. Besides, he's a nice Appaloosa once you get to know him."

I'd gotten to know Towaco when I'd worked earlier in the summer at Spidells' Stable-Mart, mucking out stalls. The Spidells run their stable like they run everything else they own in Ashland—A-Mart, Pet-Mart, Pizza-Mart. Towaco had meant no more to them than their pepperoni pizza. The gelding had developed bad habits while locked up in their stalls day and night—balking, chewing on stall wood, not coming when called. After Hawk had seen my work with Wild Thing, she had trusted me enough to finally, after weeks of arguing, convince her parents to switch Towaco to my barn. I couldn't let them down—not Hawk, and not Towaco.

Nickers quivered beneath me as we entered the field bordering our pasture. Her long, white mane blew in the warm breeze, tickling my face when I leaned forward to hug her neck. It was my last day of freedom before starting seventh grade at Ashland Middle School. I'd determined to make a name for myself no matter what it took. I wanted to stay in Ashland.

When Mom died, it felt like the hub of our family wheel had dropped out, leaving nothing but spokes with no place to go. Dad had sold our ranch in Wyoming, along with all the horses Mom had trained. The only things he kept were Lizzy and me, and sometimes I'd wondered why he kept us. Mom had been the one who kept tabs on us while Dad did his business deals. Now that he was the only parent—of two girls no less—sometimes it felt like he just didn't know what to do with us. So he didn't try. Lately things were getting better between Dad and me, since we'd finally talked about Mom's death, but we had a long way to go.

Nickers and I skimmed the border of our pasture, trees blurring by, my skin cooling in the breeze we created. Above us, geese honked as we splashed through a creek and into the pines. The sun played hide-and-seek, finger-combing the woods as if searching for Nickers and me.

As Nickers pranced through the soft pine needles, I imagined all of God's creatures watching my horse and telling the Creator what a great job he did on that white Arabian. The trail leveled off, and the scent of clover overtook the smell of pine. "Canter!" I whispered. Nickers responded so immediately I had to tighten my leg grip to stay on. Arabians have only 17 ribs, compared to 18 in other breeds, but they can outlast almost any other horse, covering 100 miles a day in endurance riding. Nickers could have kept galloping until nightfall.

We burst into a clearing, the sun shining white-hot, blinding me. Two rabbits skittered in front of us. Nickers shied, jolting to the left.

She'd calmed down a lot since I'd owned her and worked her for the past month, but she still had some rough edges.

"Whoa," I muttered, squinting until my eyes got used to the light.

Nickers stopped, snorted, and nodded. Crows cawed through the trees. Squirrels chased each other in treetops.

Thanks for making all of this, Lord, I prayed.

After Mom died, I'd gone almost two years without praying, or at least not praying much. It felt good to be on speaking terms with God again.

I leaned back and felt Nickers relax. Usually I don't let a horse graze while I'm riding because she'll get the bad habit of trying to eat during rides. But Nickers was still getting used to the no-bit bridle. I didn't have to worry about grass stains clinging to a bit, reminding her of the great taste of green and tempting her to try to graze. So I let out the rein, allowing my horse a last day's treat of summer grazing.

Nickers began pulling up tufts of clover and chomping them down.

I glanced around the open field. When I looked behind me, I saw that Nickers had snagged a branch during our ride. A stick, about a foot long, lay tangled in her silky tail. I tried to reach it but couldn't.

Nickers was content to munch meadow grass, so I threw one leg over until I sat sideways on her back. I leaned and stretched for the stick. My fingers touched it, but I couldn't grab on.

"Just keep eating, Nickers." I swung my right leg across her rump until I was sitting backwards on the mare. Leaning all the way down on her rump, I pulled her tail up with one hand and grabbed the stick with the other. "Got it!"

A whinny sounded from the woods. Nickers heard it too. She stopped grazing. A distant, uneven snort grew louder and louder. Nickers' head bobbed up. I felt her flanks tense.

"Easy, girl," I muttered. Her tail swished so that I had to hold on to it with both hands. "Wait a minute now."

A squeal pierced the clearing, swallowed by the sound of thundering hooves and human shouts as loud as the Fourth of July fireworks. In an explosion of hooves and legs, a reddish-brown, or bay, horse burst from the woods into the meadow. The rider let out a whoop, kicking his mount with both stirrups.

"Stop!" I cried, trying to wave one hand and hold on to Nickers' tail with the other. Nickers twitched. She sidestepped.

"Stay back!" I shouted, as the bay sped toward us and Nickers grew more antsy.

The rider was two horses' lengths from us when he jerked back the reins, sending his horse into a skidding stop, haunches nearly dragging the grass. Dust swirled around the bay Quarter Horse gelding, who tossed his head and struggled for balance.

Phew! I let out breath I didn't know I'd been holding. How could I have been so stupid to sit on my horse backwards, even for a second?

Nickers lifted one hoof after the other, as if the ground were on fire, but I felt her urge to bolt fade.

The bay's rider pulled off his helmet. He looked about my age, but football-player big with short brown hair. Shielding his eyes in a one-handed salute, he squinted. "You're supposed to face the other way, aren't you?" he shouted.

I could see the dimples in his cheeks from trying not to laugh. His horse looked so nervous the white star on his forehead twitched.

It wasn't funny. "And *you're* supposed to look where you're—"

But before I could finish, a shout rang out from the woods. Then came the *thuh-DUMP, thuh-DUMP* of a horse in dead gallop.

Into the clearing flew a palomino Quarter Horse, pale gold and nice-looking, but it had nowhere near the conformation, or balanced build, of the bay.

The bay's rider muttered, "Oh no."

The palomino galloped toward us. "Yo, Grant!" shouted the rider. "I'm going to beat you this time, loser!"

Nickers stirred.

The one called Grant, the bay's rider, slapped on his helmet. His horse, eager to join the race, strained against the reins and chomped the bit.

"Easy, Eager Star," I pleaded, giving the bay a name, hoping it would help.

"Gotta go!" Grant shouted, his legs stretching away from the bay's belly, prepared to deliver a kick.

"No!" I cried. "Don't—!"

Nickers' muscles tensed, bunching together like a coiled spring. I gripped her tail. "Please! You can't—!"

12

Eager Star circled in place as the palomino galloped past.

"Nobody beats me!" Grant screamed. He brought his legs down hard, digging spurs into his horse's sides. The bay reared and dropped into an instant gallop.

That did it. Nickers shot forward as if fired from a cannon. And I was in for the fastest ride of my life—backwards.

"Whoa, Nickers!" I shouted as I watched backward hoofprints form in the ground whizzing below. Riding backwards threw off my balance. I slid down Nickers' side, clinging to my handful of tail. It took all my strength to pull myself back up and straddle her flanks.

I tightened my leg grip. Nickers took it as a signal to speed up. Faster and faster she raced into the woods. Branches snapped against my back and arms. I had a backward view of the creek, the field, and finally our own pasture.

Nickers didn't slow down until she reached the barn. At the gate she stopped so short, I slid off, somehow landing on my feet.

My knees trembled. I limped up and put an

arm over Nickers' neck. *I'm okay. I made it home backwards!*

I pressed my forehead against hers, inhaling the smell of horse sweat. "Can you believe what we just did?" I blew into her nostrils and laughed. She blew back, a horse's greeting, and snorted.

"Winnie! I thought you'd never get back!" Lizzy stood a safe distance from me. She's a year younger, two inches taller, and looks enough like me to make strangers ask if we're twins. We have the same long brown hair, but Lizzy's always looks styled.

My sister feels at home with lizards, bugs, and spiders, but she's scared silly of horses. If she'd seen me galloping in backwards on Nickers, she'd have passed out on the barn floor.

"Lizzy—" I broke into laughter—"you should have seen—"

"I couldn't get Hawk to hang out and watch lizards with me. She left, and when she came back I saw who was with her! And now they're here!" she whispered, cutting me off. "And they're mad. Did you bring him back? I tried to stall. But you didn't tell me where you were going or when you'd be back or what to do when they came looking. So I—"

"Lizzy, you're not making sense." My little sister can talk faster than a Thoroughbred gallops. The only trouble Lizzy's ever gotten into at school was talking too much in class. And even then she always talked her way out of it.

My barn cat, Nelson, a gift from a friend of mine named Catman, pranced up, tail high and flicking. I picked him up. Then I saw where Lizzy was motioning with her head.

Hawk ran up to us. And right behind her came Summer Spidell, daughter of *the* Spidells of Ashland. My mind automatically imagines what breed of horse people would be if they were horses. From day one I'd pegged Summer as a yellow American Saddle Horse—not yellow as in cowardly. And not yellow-colored, although her long, blonde hair is the first thing you notice about her. And today she wore yellow shorts and a yellow spaghetti-strap T-shirt. She just makes me think yellow, a color-less, see-through personality, high-strung like a Saddle Horse. As a friend of mine would say, "No offense to the Saddle Horse."

"Where is he?" Hawk asked, worry wrinkling her forehead. Her bird flapped his wings until I put down Nelson.

"Towaco?" I asked, slipping back the knot that held the gate shut.

"Of course!" Hawk answered. "I've been so worried, Winnie!"

Summer yawned. "I tried to tell you not to put your horse here. Just look at this place."

Compared to the sleek, almost too-clean and professional Stable-Mart, our barn *did* look run-down. But unlike the Spidells' horse factory, ours was horse-friendly.

I shoved the gate open and led Nickers through. Horses, I can handle. People? That's a whole different thing.

I surveyed the pasture. No Towaco. My stomach tightened as I gave a laugh that sounded fake even to me. "Towaco's so used to being cooped up in Spidells' Stable-Mart, he's probably hiding in the barn for old time's sake."

"At least *we* always know where *our* horses are," Summer said haughtily. She unwrapped a stick of gum, folded it, and stuck it in her mouth, dropping the wrapper.

Lizzy picked up the wrapper and in a cheery voice said, "Oops. Dropped this, Summer. There you go."

Summer had no choice but to take the wrapper and say thanks.

I raced to the barn. Several wild cats streaked to the haystacks. Slanted light crisscrossed the wood floor. I ran down the stallway, calling into each stall. No Towaco.

Just great. My first customer, and I lose her horse! Winnie the Horse Loser.

Hawk and Summer followed me in.

"So?" Hawk glanced around the barn. "What have you done with my horse?"

"He—I—," I stammered.

Summer shook her head and put her arm around Hawk. "Winnie Willis, are you telling me you couldn't keep track of Victoria's horse for one hour?" Summer and her friends still called Hawk Victoria. Maybe that explained why Hawk could act like two different people sometimes.

I couldn't get words to come out. Instead, my mind flashed pictures of Towaco hovering next to the barn. That's what my mind does, whether I want it to or not. It snaps pictures that come back hours, days, even years later. They call it a photographic memory, which would be great if I had more control over which shots got taken.

Lizzy came to my rescue. "Of course Winnie hasn't lost your horse, Hawk! Towaco is . . . he's just . . ."

This was so bad, even Lizzy was having trouble explaining it away!

". . . just," Lizzy continued, ". . . misplaced. That's it!"

Summer whispered to Hawk, but I tuned them out and tried to think like Towaco: *My new home looked friendly . . . until that mare got so angry. I don't know what I did wrong. I tried to stay out of her way, but she still kicked at me. And those teeth!*

It was working. I could almost feel Towaco's fear. He'd wanted to please Nickers, but he couldn't. *The white horse left, but she'll be back. So . . .*

"Got it!" I cried. "Towaco jumped the fence when Nickers and I left."

"Got it!" echoed Hawk's bird.

"I'll bring Towaco back, and we'll start over!" I said, hoping, praying Hawk would let me.

"I'm coming with you," Hawk insisted.

I didn't want company. I figured, still thinking like a horse, that Towaco would head north, as far away from Nickers as he could get. I'd send

Hawk the other way. "Hawk, we'll find Towaco faster if we split up. You and Summer head to Stable-Mart in case Towaco goes back there. Lizzy can stay here. I'll head into town."

"That's the first good idea I've heard all day," Summer said, sneering. "If Towaco has a brain, he'll head back to *our* stable, where he won't get roughed up by wild horses."

"Go!" Lizzy's fence lizard, Larry, poked its head from her shirt pocket. "Larry and I will keep a lookout here."

"I don't know . . ." Hawk looked torn.

Summer tugged Hawk in the direction of Stable-Mart. "Don't worry, Victoria. *We'll* get everything back to normal."

I wheeled out the back bike, Dad's backward bicycle invention, and pushed it across our junky yard, filled with "works-in-progress," as Dad calls the broken appliances dumped off for him to repair. With all the inventions Dad worked on, it hadn't taken long for him to get the title Odd-Job Willis in town.

Once in the street, I hopped on the bike, which looks normal. It goes forward, but only when you pedal backwards, which is what I did as fast as I could.

"Towaco!" For two blocks I called, but no sign of him. I sniffed. The sweet smell of manure let me know I was on the right track.

In front of Pat's Pets, I slammed on the brakes— first backward, making me go faster, then front-ward. Pat Haven had given me a job working the computer pet help line. That was where I got to know Barker and Catman. Pat hired them for the help line too. She'd help me find Towaco.

The door opened, and down the steps came Catman Coolidge, walking like he was made of rubber. Catman's a year older than I am, but he looks a lot older. With his long, wavy blond hair, fringed flairs, and tie-dyed shirt, he looked like a hippie from the 60s and 70s.

"Catman!" I shouted.

He squinted his amazing Siamese-blue, cat-shaped eyes from behind gold, wire-rimmed glasses and held up a two-fingered *V*, the peace sign. Usually he wears sandals, but today he was barefoot.

"Catman, I lost Hawk's horse!"

"Far out," he said, no hint of a grin.

I walked the bike to him. "If I don't find that horse fast, Hawk might take him back to Stable-Mart. And Towaco—"

Catman raised one finger to shush me. "Found him."

"What—?" But I stopped.

A car honked, then another, long and angry. The honking was coming from Claremont and Main, the busiest intersection in Ashland.

"Barker!" Catman whistled through his fingers.

Around the corner came Eddy Barker, led by three dogs that looked like a canine version of The Three Bears—big, middle-sized, and wee. Barker wore a Cleveland Indians baseball cap backwards and shades. His skin was the color of the big, chocolate Lab straining at the leash. "Winnie! Horse! Downtown!"

I dropped my bike and took off running, praying Towaco would be okay. Barker's dogs barked at my heels. Catman passed me. Horns blared.

We rounded the corner. There in the exact center of the intersection stood Towaco, statue still, as if he couldn't hear the horns.

But I knew he heard them.

Crowds gathered on the sidewalk, some shouting, some laughing. I wanted to cry for Towaco.

"Careful, Winnie!" Barker called.

I was still weaving among cars when I saw Catman ahead, circling the air with his peace sign. Miraculously one car pulled out of line, circled back, and drove off. The next car did the same, and the next, clearing out a whole lane.

Meanwhile Barker and his dogs moved back and forth, calming traffic like a crossing guard.

I inched toward Towaco. "You're a brave horse!"

Towaco's glassy eyes stared past me. He didn't flinch when I took hold of his halter.

"You're a good horse for standing still." Mom taught me you can always find something to praise a horse for.

Ninety-nine percent of the horses I meet will follow me, but Towaco's legs seemed glued to the street. One problem Hawk wanted me to work her horse through was balking.

So is this my chance, God?

Someone yelled out a car window. I glanced up in time to see Catman raise his thumb and pinkie, the Hawaiian sign for "hang loose."

"Think about something else, Towaco." Gently I tucked the tip of his ear under the top of his halter. It wouldn't hurt, but it could make him wonder.

After a few seconds, Towaco's eyes came back into focus. He shook his head. The ear flicked up. I had my chance, and I took it, tugging him sideways. He followed me, switching flies with his tail as if nothing else mattered.

"Thanks!" I yelled to Barker and Catman as they handled the last of the traffic.

And thanks, God!

I led Towaco past Pat's Pets to my street. Winnie the Horse Gentler was back in business!

Or not.

There in our yard was my dad, arms folded. Next to him stood Summer, hands on hips. Hawk was wiping away tears. And Hawk's mother glared at me as if I were a horse thief. Looming at the curb was the trailer, tailgate down and ready, waiting to take Towaco away.

*H*awk hugged her horse while Mrs. Hawkins checked the gelding for injuries.

Lizzy did most of the talking for my side, while Dad made little disapproving noises that made my stomach ache.

When she'd finished her inspection, Hawk's mom turned to Hawk. "Your horse seems to be in one piece, Victoria. Shall we load him?"

My grip tightened on Towaco's halter. "Please, Hawk." My voice cracked, and I swallowed. "I'm so sorry! It won't happen again."

Summer made a *harrrumph.*

Mrs. Hawkins, who looks more like a brown-haired Summer than she does Hawk, glanced at the pasture, then back to her daughter. "I think we should move the horse back to Stable-Mart, but I'll leave the decision to you."

"Hawk, I can help Towaco. I know I can! Please give me another chance." Inside I was making the same plea to God.

"You won't be sorry!" Lizzy promised. "You know Winnie rocks with horses!"

Hawk stroked Towaco under his mane. He'd relaxed so much his eyelids almost shut when she scratched him. She kept silent a full minute before she spoke. "Towaco can stay—but only if Wild Thing stops frightening him!"

I fought the urge to remind her that my horse's name is Nickers, not Wild Thing. But Hawk was saving my skin. "Thanks, Hawk!"

Mrs. Hawkins left with Hawk, Summer, and an empty trailer. I was getting a second chance, and I better not blow it. I needed another client, another horse to gentle. I sure couldn't afford to lose the one I already had.

Lizzy ran inside to get dinner.

Dad still hadn't said anything to me, if you don't count sighs. He followed me to the pasture and opened the gate. I knew it was costing him not to bawl me out. He didn't need to. I felt lousy enough. Lizzy says our dad is handsome for an old person, but I don't know. He's tall, thin, with curly black hair that gets pretty scraggly before he thinks about a haircut.

"Winnie . . ." Dad opened his mouth, then shut it. "Don't be long."

I watched Dad shuffle away.

As soon as I turned Towaco loose, Nickers protested, snorting and squealing. Poor Towaco tried being friendly, backing off, squealing back—everything. But in Nickers' eyes, the Appaloosa could do nothing right.

I knew just how Towaco felt.

"I can't wait for school tomorrow!" Lizzy exclaimed as Dad and I munched quietly on the tuna patties she'd molded into turtles. "Remember that green shirt I haven't worn in a year? I stitched the collar down and hemmed it short. It rocks with my khakis! How about you, Winnie? What are you wearing your first day of seventh grade?"

"Haven't thought about it," I answered truthfully.

"Winnie!" Lizzy cried. "How could you not have thought about it?"

I set down my fork and glanced at Dad. "Guess I was worried about other stuff."

"What other stuff?" Lizzy demanded.

"Like . . . getting a reputation as a great horse gentler." *One who doesn't lose horses anyway.*

"Sweet!" Lizzy squeezed my arm. "A new school is like the perfect place for getting a reputation! You can be anybody you want! It's a do-over!"

A picture flashed into my mind of the only time I'd seen Mom thrown from a horse. She'd bought an abused buckskin off some horse trader. Lizzy toddled out to the training pen. Mom turned to see her, and that was all the excuse the buckskin needed. The mare bucked a series of hard, twisted kicks, and Mom flew to the dirt. She sat in the dust for several minutes. Then she got up, walked straight to that horse, looked her in the eyes, said "Do-over," and got back on. The buckskin ended up being her favorite mount. It was the first horse Dad sold after Mom died.

"A do-over," I repeated. In a way I'd been bucked off most of the schools we'd attended in the *I* states. Well, not really. I just never seemed to fit in. Making new friends had been so hard, it was just easier to do things alone.

Dad looked up. "Listen to Lizzy, honey."

I knew what Dad was saying: *Be more like Lizzy this time—adored by teachers and students.* Dad had never gotten a call from one of Lizzy's teachers, asking him to come in and discuss *her*. Not that Dad didn't love me as much as Lizzy. I knew he did. Lizzy's just easier. Mom told me once that Dad had been so sure I'd be a boy, my name had almost been William. So I guess I'd disappointed him from day one.

"Bet lots of kids around here have horses," Dad said, talking to Lizzy instead of me. "Some of them must have problems—the horses, I mean." Dad turned to me. "But schoolwork comes first. Maybe taking on another horse would be too much."

"No way! I've been working with Towaco, even while he was still at Stable-Mart. He's easy." Anyway, Mom and I had gentled a dozen at once.

Dad sighed and scooted his chair back. "Well, I think I'll see if I can get my cat horn working, a little invention Catman and I are working on.

Did you know that Einstein invented the cat door? Catman told me. Maybe I should give him a call and see if he wants to help."

"Dad?" Lizzy scraped leftover tuna turtle into a plastic bag while I cleared the table.

"Maybe I should work on my automatic table-clearing machine," Dad mumbled. "Did you know the dishwasher was invented by the wife of an Illinois politician, and not because she hated doing dishes? Her servants kept breaking her china and—"

Lizzy interrupted. "Dad, shouldn't you make calls first?"

Dad had just taken an extra job until one of his inventions caught on, or until he got more odd-job work like the projects already sitting in our yard. Mr. Spidell had turned him down on stocking the back bike at A-Mart. So my dad, who hadn't used a cellular phone since he quit his insurance job in Wyoming, had to call strangers and convince them life was not complete without a cell phone.

Dad's face sagged as if the muscles had snapped. "You're right."

I wanted to make him feel better. "And you're right about school, Dad!" I forced a smile.

"I'll make those teachers and kids crazy about me! Some of them are bound to hire me to gentle their horses! You'll see."

But my mind shot photos to my brain of the kids at the last school, where everybody but me knew the secret codes. *This is in, that's not. That's cool, that's dumb.*

"Too bad it's not a school for horses though," I muttered when I thought Dad was out of hearing. "Horses are so much easier to understand than humans."

Dad bounded back into the kitchen. "Eureka, Winnie! All you have to do is think of those students as horses! Teachers too, only I wouldn't let them know. Treat them like you do your horses, and they'll stampede to your barn!"

The next morning I woke up at five and couldn't get back to sleep.

Lizzy, already dressed, stood humming over a pan of hash browns. The humming stopped when I walked in decked out in my old blue jeans and a ratty T-shirt. "Winnie! You can't wear that!"

I grinned. "I'm going for a ride, Lizzy."

"But—"

"I'll be back in plenty of time. I'll wear anything you pick out for me, okay?" Not that there was much to pick from. Each time we moved, we left more stuff behind, parts of ourselves, shedding our skins like snakes.

In minutes Nickers and I were cantering through a morning dipped in dew, her hoof-beats the drums to overhead geese. This was my world, the only time I felt totally okay.

But I'd have to make middle school my world too. For the first time, I really cared about making a good impression. People had to get to know Winnie the Horse Gentler.

The sun was up by the time we trotted back home. Towaco whinnied and came in for oats. He seemed more at home. I didn't think it would take long to work out his kinks, now that he was free from Stable-Mart.

"You're back!" Lizzy cried when the screen door slammed behind me. "Dad knew you'd be late, but you're not! I set out your best jeans and that turquoise shirt. Brings out the green in your eyes."

When I came out of the shower, I heard Dad

banging on something outside. Another invention. Lizzy had my backpack loaded with three notebooks and a brown bag.

"Thanks for packing me a lunch, Lizzy." I tried not to think about the notes Mom used to drop into our lunch boxes, how I'd hide them under my napkin. "I wish sixth through eighth grades were together like in Wyoming. At least we'd be in the same building."

"It's a short week, Winnie. You'll do fine!"

That part I liked, starting on the Wednesday before Labor Day. It gave us three days on, then three days off to get over it.

Lizzy pulled on her orange backpack. "Sweet! I'm off."

Lizzy had always been the first kid to school, waiting for the doors to open. I still needed to fix my hair.

As I was leaving, Dad climbed into his truck. We'd sold our car in Wyoming and crossed the country in the cattle truck. It took all of Dad's inventor skills to keep the thing running.

"Winnie? I thought you'd left already!" The engine caught on the third try. Exhaust fumes shot up like thunderclouds.

"Plenty of time!" I shouted, waving. *I haven't blown it yet, Dad.*

He waved back, and the truck jerked forward, then chugged off down the street. Lizzy had stuck on a new bumper sticker: *We brake for bugs!*

From the pasture came a sharp whinny. Nickers neighed. I couldn't leave without checking on the horses. I dropped my bike and ran.

Nickers and Towaco stood a horse's length apart. Nickers, ears flicking, stuck out her muzzle, flared nostrils at Towaco. She was trying to make friends!

But Towaco didn't understand. He took off in a dead run to the back of the pasture. Nickers whinnied, trying to call him back. But when Towaco kept running, Nickers bucked, offended, then tore out after the Appaloosa.

"Nickers, no!" I called.

I climbed the fence, snagging my shirt on the way over, and ran through the wet grass after the horses. When I caught up with Nickers, she looked rejected, and Towaco scared.

"You two!" I scratched Nickers' withers. It was almost funny. My horse was as bad at horse relationships as I was with people relationships.

36

"Nickers, maybe you should think of horses as people."

People! School!

I ran through the pasture, over the fence, across the yard, to the back bike.

I didn't see another kid on the street. Maybe they were all early, like Lizzy.

Nobody could have pedaled faster. But when I reached middle school, only a couple of grown-ups were hanging outside. I shoved my bike into the full rack, next to Catman's back bike. Even Catman was here!

Sweat puddled under my arms as I raced up the steps of Ashland Middle School and into the halls—the empty halls. The sloshing of my soggy tennis shoes echoed as I tiptoed toward the classrooms.

Way to go, Winnie! Late for the first day of school.

*R*emember, I told myself, searching frantically through my pocket for my class schedule. *These students are just a bunch of horses. And you're just looking for your first herd.*

But even horses worry about first impressions. A new horse tries to come off strong and confident.

Found it! I unfolded the schedule. Room 228.

Taking the stairs two at a time, I reached second floor, expecting to get yelled at for prowling the halls.

Voices floated from classrooms. One teacher with black bangs and a long face stuck her head out of her classroom. I imagined a black mare sticking her head out of her stall as I tiptoed past.

Room 228. I yanked out my rubber band, since most of my ponytail had straggled out anyway. Taking a deep breath, I went in.

The "lead mare" stopped talking as I moved to the front row, where the only empty seats were.

"Winnie!" someone whispered.

Amazed to hear my name, I glanced up and saw Eddy Barker waving me over.

"Barker!" I plopped into the seat next to him. "Is this English?"

Before Barker could answer, the teacher tapped my desk.

I looked up into the angular face of a middle-aged woman with tiny, gray eyes and red lines for lips. Her olive suit matched her shoes and skin, as if she'd dipped herself into a can of paint. I stared too long, imagining what breed she'd be if she were a horse.

"Miss . . . I'm afraid I don't know your name since you chose not to join us for introductions."

She didn't say it mean. More like disappointed. Her forehead wrinkled like a worried Barb, a North African desert horse. Barbs might even have been around longer than Arabians.

"Sorry," I said.

She kept frowning at me, as if waiting for something.

"My name? Winnie . . . Winnie . . . Willis," I stammered. *Winnie the Horse Gentler. Maybe you've heard of me?* But I couldn't say it for real.

"I marked a Winifred Willis absent earlier." She picked up her grade book.

Someone snickered behind me. I turned to see Summer Spidell in the back row, whispering something to Hawk.

Another kid whispered, "Odd-Job Willis."

I turned back around but caught a glimpse of somebody I'd seen before. *No way!* I peeked again, then slumped in my seat. *Grant! The kid on Eager Star. The one who spooked Nickers and sent me on a backward ride!*

And I'd have bet three Shetland ponies that he was telling everybody about seeing me ride backwards! I could imagine what they were saying—backward bike, backward horse . . . backward girl.

The teacher cleared her throat, which is what some people do without realizing it after I talk, like clearing their throats will make me sound less gravelly. "I'm Ms. Brumby."

Brumby? She had to be kidding. A Brumby is

41

a bony, Roman-nosed, Australian scrub horse, disagreeable and hard to train. I stared at her frizzed hair, bony face, large nose—a Brumby! All my emotions sucked together and came out with the force of a horse's kick, a burst of laughter that sprayed spit.

Barker stared at me, wide-eyed.

The room stilled.

"Do you find my name so amusing, Miss Willis?" she asked coldly, turning her grade book in her arms. The cover had an address label on it and big, black letters that read BARB BRUMBY.

No! Not Barb! A Barb is a tough, desert horse, the one I'd thought of when I first saw her. I tried to stifle the laugh that pressed against my ribs, making my eyes water. *Barb Brumby!*

Barker elbowed me, as if I needed a heads-up that I was sinking myself.

"Sorry—" I choked on the word and stared at my desk.

"Miss Willis," Ms. Brumby said evenly, "we do serious work in this class. You would be advised to get here on time from now on."

I nodded, not trusting myself to speak.

As she laid out her class plans, I pulled myself

together. First class, first teacher, first impression. How could I have blown it already?

I managed to tune in to class again. "One-third of your grade will come from your journals. You're free to write whatever you desire."

Right. I already knew I'd be keeping two journals—a fake one for her, and a real one for me. Like I'd want Ms. Brumby to know what I *really* thought of her class or of life in Ashland Middle School.

I did like journal-keeping though. When I was nine, Mom and I took a three-day ride into the hills to observe a herd of wild Mustangs. We camped out, getting up with the sun just to watch horses all day. I'd kept a journal, recording how they jockeyed for position in the herd.

I got an idea. I pulled out two of my notebooks. While Ms. Brumby talked, I opened the gray notebook, closest in color to Nickers, for my real journal. In the red notebook I'd write what the teacher wanted to hear.

On the gray cover I wrote: *Ashland Middle School.* Then I began:

The horses at middle school divide into small herds, where each horse struggles to make a strong

first impression. A social order exists, with low strag-
glers and high horses ignoring each other.

From the back row some girl snorted, and I heard Summer's fake giggle.

Mares have been known to make weird noises to be noticed by the stallions, I wrote. *False whinnies and snorts can—*

I shut my notebook as Ms. Brumby walked up. A buzzer sounded, and kids didn't wait to be excused. "For tomorrow, class, read the nursery rhymes in chapter one of your text for the intro-duction to our poetry unit. I expect intelligent discussion." She glanced at me, her lips turned up slightly, as if to say, *I don't expect it from you.*

"You have math now?" Barker shouted. Kids exited classrooms in a giant student stampede.

"Yeah!" I yelled, relieved to have him in another class.

Lizzy babysits for Barker's five brothers, and she thinks they're the nicest people on earth. Barker's dad teaches poetry at Ashland Univer-sity. But he doesn't look like a poet. He played AU football as a student. Mrs. Barker teaches computer science at the same university. I bet they eat lunch together every day.

Our math teacher, Treadwater—known as

Mr. T. reminded me of a pony we'd trained in Wyoming. He was short, with a scraggly gray beard and a face that would have looked at home on Mt. Rushmore. He got so excited about numbers I didn't understand half of what he said. As he talked about the beauty of basic single digits, I pictured him pawing the floor, horse counting *1, 2, 3.*

My last class before lunch was life science. On the blackboard was a list of animals:

Mayfly—24 hrs
Hamster—1.8 yrs
Bat—2 yrs
Black Salamander—3 yrs
Mouse—3 yrs
Tick—3–4 yrs
Blue Jay—4 yrs
Blue Spider—15 yrs
Goat—18 yrs
Cat—21 yrs
Macaw—64 yrs
Box Turtle—123 yrs
Giant Tortoise—177 yrs

At the bottom, it said:

Bristlecone Pines—thousands of yrs
Humans—eternity?

Then I saw the title at the top of the list: *Longest Known Life Spans*.

Cool! There just might be one class I'd like at AMS.

Summer and Grant walked in together. I grabbed a seat under the window at the opposite side of the room.

Hawk glided in, her multicolored dress catching the light so it sparkled. Every guy in the room looked up.

"Victoria!" a tall, sandy blond guy called out. Then I recognized him as the palomino rider who'd been racing Grant.

Terrific. Now Grant and his racing buddy could compare notes about me.

Hawk's gaze met mine, and she nodded slightly as she took her seat next to Summer. I guess I should have known she'd be Summer's "Victoria" at school, not my "Hawk." I couldn't really blame her. You couldn't just pull away from a kid like Summer if you wanted to stay in her group—the popular group.

Grant and Summer were play-fighting over a pen.

Kids grew louder, and still no sign of a teacher.

"Man!" said Grant's buddy, getting to his feet. "That stuff on the board looks hard!" He slid between chairs to the board and started erasing. "No way do I want some teach making me memorize all this!"

"Go, Brian!" yelled a redheaded girl in a tank top. "My hero!"

A couple of kids clapped. Summer giggled.

Outside in the hall, something clattered to the ground. Brian dropped the eraser and darted back to his seat.

"Rats!" came the voice from the hall. Papers shuffled. "No offense."

No offense? Only one person excused herself to rats. But Pat Haven ran Pat's Pets, the pet store where I worked. She didn't teach school.

Yet in she came, carrying a pile of papers high as a haystack. Her short, brown curls bounced. She's a miniature horse, compact and springy.

"Can you believe I got lost?" she exclaimed. "I was here before school started this morning, but things look different with all you kids in the building. I've been running around like a chicken with its head cut off! No offense."

"No offense for what?" Brian asked.

Pat dumped her papers onto the teacher's

desk. "To the chickens! More of them than there are of us." She took a deep breath and looked around the room. When she saw me, she winked.

"You're not Mr. Scott," said the guy next to me. He wore glasses, khaki pants, and a navy T-shirt under a green-checked shirt.

"Why, you're sharp as a porcupine, aren't you?" Pat smiled at him until he blushed. "No offense to our quill-filled friends. I'm Ms. Haven, your substitute until Mr. Scott returns."

"I know you!" shouted the redhead. "You're the lady from Pat's Pets."

"Give that lady a gold star!" Pat shouted back.

This was too weird. Why hadn't she told me she'd be teaching?

"Will everything you teach be on Mr. Scott's final, Mrs. Haven?" Grant asked politely.

"Let's not worry about the final our first day of class! Today we'll talk about life! Life Science. How long is life? you ask." She stared around the room, her big, brown eyes holding everyone captive. "It all depends. Take a look-see." Pat wheeled around to face the board and her shoulders sagged. Until that instant, she must not have noticed that all her work had been erased. I felt so sorry for her, so angry at Brian and his buddies, I considered ratting them out. No offense.

$\mathcal{P}$at stared at the blank board. She rifled through her papers. "If I had a brain in my head, I'd have typed that list instead of copying it onto the board this morning. Now you don't have it. And neither do I."

I could tell she didn't know what to do with us now.

"I remember nightingales can live three years, although most don't . . ." Her voice trailed off.

I couldn't stand seeing her struggle, especially since it was Brian's fault. Ordinarily, I'd have kept my mouth shut and waited for the class to end. But Pat had been great to Lizzy and me and Dad since we moved to Ashland. She'd rented us our house, sent Dad repair work, and given me a job on the pet help line.

Besides, wasn't this year supposed to be different?

"I can put your list back up," I offered, my voice hoarser than normal.

Pat perked up like a mare seeing her weaned foal. "You copied it already?"

"Not exactly." I moved to the board. For once, maybe my photographic memory could come in handy.

Even though Brian had left nothing but a few swirls of chalk dust, when I stared at the board, I could see the list as clearly as if it were still there. My mind had taken a photo. I never know how long photos will stick in my brain, which makes it hard to count on my memory for tests. But for now, I could see everything. I just filled in what I saw as I wrote:

Mayfly—24 hrs
Hamster—1.8 yrs
Bat—2 yrs
Black Salamander—3 yrs
Mouse—3 yrs
Tick—3–4 yrs
Blue Jay—4 yrs

I kept writing, hoping Pat would break the silence behind me and start talking again.

Blue Spider—15 yrs
Goat—18 yrs
Cat—21 yrs

"Well, I'll be a blue-nosed gopher!" Pat exclaimed. "No offense. Winnie, you remembered all those numbers just right. Don't forget, everybody. These aren't average life spans. These are the oldest known ages."

No kidding. I'd never known a horse to reach 62, but that's what I wrote by *Horse*. Mom said when she was a kid, horses hardly ever topped 20 years. With better feed for older horses now, you can expect your horse to live 20, even 30, years. I hoped Nickers would break the 62-year record.

Pat talked about the class, but I didn't hear much. I kept writing until I got to the end and circled *eternity* the way she had. Then I sat back down.

"What's with eternity?" Summer asked. "I don't get it."

"That's a shame, Summer," Pat said, her voice light. "I'm hoping we can talk more about that one."

"Is all of this going to be on the test?" Grant asked, scribbling furiously.

"What test?" Pat asked. "Oh, can't say. But I'm sure y'all want to copy the list Winnie so graciously recopied for us."

Brian groaned.

Kids flipped open notebooks, bummed paper, dug for pens.

I copied the list too, just in case the photograph wasn't the long-lasting kind. I'd just written *eternity* when the buzzer rang.

Kids rushed out faster than ever for lunch.

The tall, redheaded girl stopped in front of my seat. "That was so tight! If I had your memory, I'd never crack a book! Not that I do now."

"Thanks!" *Unreal! Somebody's talking to me on the first day of school? I made a good first impression? What if she has a horse and—?*

"I'm Salena. Call me Sal."

Summer walked up behind Sal and shoved her toward the door. "And you can call *her* Pat's Pet."

Sal laughed, elbowed Summer, then walked out with her.

Hawk drifted past. "See you at lunch, Winnie." But she didn't wait for me.

I stepped out into the hall and slipped behind

the door, pressed to the bricks, waiting for an opening among the students. Taking out my gray notebook, I observed the herd galloping to the cafeteria. Hawk kept step with Summer and Sal.

Established mares don't like to associate with new mares who might not fit into their herd, I wrote. *They prance and strut with the popular mares, ignoring the new mare.*

The three girls stopped to let Grant catch up. I observed how things changed. Summer and Sal tried to talk to Grant at the same time, competing for his attention. Mom and I had observed the exact same thing in the herd of Mustangs we'd watched.

Mares turn on each other, I continued, *as soon as a male enters the herd. They'll sacrifice female friendship in hopes of snagging the male.*

"Split for lunch?" Catman strode by, the first time I'd seen him at school. He didn't slow down, so I hoisted my pack and trotted after him.

"Ever think," he shouted, not turning around, "that the hokeypokey *is* what it's all about?"

Sometimes you have to ignore the Catman.

The cafeteria was as noisy as an auction barn. Catman tossed his rainbow-colored pack on a table and headed for the food line.

I pulled out the lunch Lizzy had packed.
Nobody sat at my table, although every other
table seemed crowded. I looked around for
Barker but didn't see him. Grant and Summer
plunked their trays at the table behind me.
Hawk sat across from Summer.

Nothing but horses. I'd have to break in sooner
or later if I wanted to get known around here.
I'd face Grant, let him ridicule me for riding
backwards, and then get on with it.

Only not now. I pretended to study my
peanut-butter-and-cheese sandwich.

I peeked at Summer's table. Grant swiveled,
tapped his spoon, surveyed the cafeteria, waving
over a couple of kids—the king granting favors.

Grant is herd leader, I wrote in my journal.
*Anyone who wants to move up in the social order
around here has to impress him. Acceptance by the
leader brings acceptance by the herd.*

And I'd made a lousy first impression on
Grant.

Grant fork-banged his tray, jiggled in his seat,
ate too fast.

I wrote: *Grant's what's known as a "hot" horse—
an eager, nervous creature who chews on the bit, runs
instead of lopes, and can't stand still under saddle.*

"Type A personality?" Catman plopped down his tray across from me. "My great-grandfather was in the army. He's type A."

I snapped my journal shut. "How long were you standing there, Catman?"

"Long enough. Horses—people—far out."

"I'm trying to understand them," I admitted. "I need more problem horses, so I've got to get to know kids like Grant and his group."

Catman scraped up watery applesauce from the corner square of his tray. I didn't know if he'd heard me or not.

"See that?" I pointed, and Catman looked just as Summer ruffled up Grant's hair. "Touch. It's the way horses communicate. Humans too, I guess."

I pointed to the clusters of kids around the cafeteria. "There! Zebras hang out in threes like that. Those six girls and one guy—a Przewalski harem—six mares to one stallion." I bit into my sandwich. "I wish humans were as easy to understand as horses. Horses say more with their ears than most people do with their mouths. Nickers has 16 muscles that move her ears in all directions to let me know exactly how she feels."

"Cats have 32," Catman said. He drank his

chocolate milk in one gulp. He'd eaten everything on his plate, plus Lizzy's lizard-shaped oatmeal cookies I'd donated.

Summer and Hawk stood up in the center of their noisy group, which included Brian and Sal. Side by side, the two seventh-graders looked like opposites. Hawk was as dark as Summer was light, brown eyes and black hair to Summer's gray eyes and blonde hair. But they had two things in common—both were lead mares, and every stallion in this herd was attracted to them.

"That's the group I have to break into," I whispered to Catman as they walked past our table.

"Grant!" Catman shouted.

The peanut butter stuck in my throat.

"Catman?" Grant sounded surprised.

"Somebody here you ought to meet." Catman waved his hand toward me.

Run! Flee! It's a horse's natural response to terror, which is what I felt. I refused to look up.

"Oh?" Grant sounded puzzled, cautious, as if he thought Catman might be tricking him.

Catman scraped the last drop of tapioca from his tray. "Winnie Willis."

Nowhere to run. No place to hide. Face Grant

right now. Take my punishment, the teasing. Get it over with. Move on. A do-over.

I looked up, bracing myself to be mocked out.

Grant waved to someone behind me. Then he studied me up and down as if checking my conformation, considering the purchase, rejecting me as unsound. "I'm Grant."

I waited.

Nothing.

No sign of recognition.

I couldn't speak. It felt like Grant could see through me to something more interesting on the other side of the cafeteria.

"Come on, Grant!" Summer tugged his arm. Hawk walked ahead.

"See you, Catman," Grant called back.

I stared at his back as he walked away. Everything I'd imagined he'd say, the ribbing I'd have to take—it hadn't come. He hadn't teased me because he hadn't noticed me.

Why should I worry about making a bad first impression? I couldn't even *make* an impression!

𝒜fternoon classes dragged on. Social studies and keyboarding sounded like work. Art and gym weren't so bad because we just talked about doing stuff and didn't really do anything.

After school, kids ran from the building as if it were on fire.

"I switched into Pat's class," Barker shouted as we fought for our bikes. Kids jerked the rack, yelling across the street or down the sidewalk. "Pat didn't even know she was subbing until yesterday. She said Mr. Scott needed time off for 'middle-school syndrome.'"

I didn't know what it was, but I suspected I had it too. And I'd only been in middle school one day.

Catman whisked through the masses on his

back bike. "Stop by my pad? Say hey to Churchill?" Churchill is the father of Nelson, the cat Catman gave me. Catman named them after Winston Churchill and his wartime cat, Nelson.

I was glad not to have to go home and face Dad. He'd want to hear about my new friends and their problem horses. Couldn't hurt putting off his disappointment.

A dozen cats ran out of bushes to greet us as Barker, Catman, and I left our bikes at the foot of Catman's lane. Catman slid his glasses on top of his head so he could nuzzle three tabby kittens.

Flat-faced Churchill plodded up to me.

"How goes the war?" I asked, stroking his back until it arched.

Catman stood up. *"Keeeeee-y!"*

Cat Burglar, white with a black mask, darted past us. Wilhemina, the fat orange tabby, and a dozen others followed as we walked up the overgrown lane. A beautiful, longhaired, white cat threaded through my feet, almost tripping me. "Who's White Beauty here?"

"Haven't you met Aussie?" Catman asked in an Australian accent. "Great cat lovers, them Aussies. Number one cat-owning country in the world. Canada's second, U.S. third."

Coolidge Castle loomed ahead, the roof shooting off in every direction, ending in a spire. Most of the windows were boarded up, and the whole house looked like it had waited 200 years for a coat of paint. Looking at it, nobody would ever guess that inside velvet furniture covered wood floors and chandeliers hung over a living room as big as a paddock.

Mr. Coolidge appeared on the weedy lawn. He was carrying a plastic figure that looked a little like him—shortish, with plastic hair that resembled his hairpiece. "Sa-a-ay!" he called, setting down the statue. "What did the teacher say when I hammered my thumb?" He taped a hammer to the statue's hands and lined it next to six other figures, some with shovels, others with brooms. *"Smart, Bart?"* Bart Coolidge laughed so hard it sounded like a draft horse whinny. Smart Bart's is his used-car business. He must have dreamed of being a comedian because he's got a million corny jokes, one for every occasion.

"I like your seven dwarves, Mr. Coolidge!" Barker yelled.

"For Labor Day," Catman whispered. "Hi ho, off to work. Get it? My parents are very big on lawn ornaments."

"Stop on down to Smart Bart's if you *really* want decorations!" Mr. Coolidge patted his hairpiece. "Sa-a-ay! What did one headlight say to the other?"

I started laughing already. "I give."

"I'm brighter than you are!" He laughed so hard I stepped back. His Scooby Doo vest looked so tight. I didn't want to be around when a button blew.

We followed Catman inside.

Mrs. Coolidge shouted from the winding staircase, "Calvin!" as if he'd been lost. She wore pink stretch pants, and her bright yellow hair was piled high as a beehive.

She ran up to me and in one motion twisted my hair up off my neck. "I would give my right arm for this hair, wouldn't you, Barker? I told the girls at the salon about your thick, wavy brown, dear. You have to stop in and prove Claire Coolidge is no liar!"

She sat us at the mile-long table and fed us cookies and purple drinks in skinny glasses with paper umbrellas. Catman downed 14 cookies, eating the outside of each cookie first and then the filling.

I leaned back in the carved throne chair and

enjoyed how cool the house felt with the heavy, red curtains drawn and blocking out heat and light.

Mr. Coolidge burst into the house and kissed his wife. Two of his vest buttons were missing. "I was talking with the boys at the Ashland business meeting about the future of our town. Calvin, did you declare a career today?"

"A career?" I asked, trying to picture Catman selling used cars.

"Eighth-grade project," Barker explained. "They have to research a career all year for a big report."

Catman licked filling from his lips. "Telegraph operator."

"As in the Morse code?" Barker asked. "Dash . . . dash . . . dash?"

"Yep." Catman peeled two bananas at the same time.

Mr. Coolidge frowned. "Sa-a-ay! I don't think they have telegraphs *or* operators anymore."

Catman got his catlike grin. "Groovy. No competition."

"A person must make a name in this world!" declared Catman's dad. "Isn't that so, Mrs. Coolidge? We all need a reputation!"

I had to agree with him. "I could sure use a reputation as a horse whisperer. I just don't know where to start."

"Start right here, young Winifred!" He patted my head. "Join the Ashland Business Association!"

Wow! "Would they let me?"

"Decidedly not!" he admitted. "But what of your father? Getting the Willis name about town would serve your purpose. It would be my great honor to invite him to our luncheon!"

"No kidding?" It was a step. Maybe Summer would stop making fun of Odd-Job Willis. "Thanks!"

Later that afternoon Catman, Barker, and I took turns answering the pet help line at Pat's Pets. I let Barker and Catman answer dog and cat e-mails first. I still wasn't in a hurry to face Dad.

As Barker wrote to someone called K-9, I read over his shoulder:

> I've tried everything to get my poodle to heel! I jerk the leash and drag her. I

tried hitting her when she wouldn't
obey (not hard enough to hurt!) and
shaking her to get her attention.
—K-9

Around us, birds squawked and dogs barked
as Barker wrote his answer:

Dear K-9,
　　You AND your dog will get more out
of this relationship if you praise your dog
instead of punishing her! Find things she
does right and praise her. Dogs are
pleasers! I'll bet yours loves you no matter what. Why don't you do the same?
—Barker

Pat finished with a customer and joined us
at the computer center. "You got me out of a
pickle today, Winnie! Don't know what I'd done
if you hadn't written my notes back up on the
board! Lizzy said you had a photographic
memory. I guess you do!" Her denim overalls
made it hard to believe she was our teacher.

While Catman took over at the keyboard, Pat
talked with Barker and me. I'd been afraid that
having her as a teacher would ruin her as my
friend. But she was the same Pat.

I waited while Catman answered a kid who was worried about his Russian blue cat having six toes, and another kid whose cat kept climbing his mother's plants.

Finally it was my turn. I love having people I don't even know e-mail me at the help line and ask for my help with their horses. I'd probably mess it up if I had to give them advice face-to-face. I tackled the first e-mail:

Dear Winnie,

My horse is barn sour! He's no fun anymore. I have to fight him, kicking and flicking the reins to get him to ride away from the barn. Coming back is great, as long as I don't try to make him go anywhere but straight home. I'm tired of it. Should I get a new horse?
—Tall in the Saddle

Dear Tall in the Saddle,

Don't give up your horse! I'll bet he hates disappointing you. When's the last time you told him what a great horse he is? See, what you're doing is punishing your horse (kicking, flicking) for heading away from the barn.

(Would you want to go somewhere when you knew you'd get kicked all along the way?) And you're probably rewarding him for racing to the barn by feeding him there. Instead, praise him as you ride away from the barn. Then feed him when you're out there. Love him every step of the way!
—Winnie

As I left Pat's Pets, I tried to think of something to tell Dad about my day. I'd promised this year would be different, and so far it wasn't. Lizzy said new schools let you start over and be anybody you wanted to be. But it didn't work that way for me. Every school was different, but I wasn't. I still got the same quivering stomach when a teacher called on me, when I walked into the lunchroom, or when I stepped into the crowded hall. All I'd wanted to do was bolt like a Mustang.

Instead of going into the house, I worked with Towaco for an hour. It paid off. Every time he did something right, I praised him. And that made him want to please me all the more.

The sun had set by the time I finished a quick

ride on Nickers. Lightning bugs signaled, flashing on and off as I finished mucking stalls.

I was hurrying to the house when Lizzy stood up from behind a bush. "Look! I found a friend for Larry!" She pointed to a log, where her latest find—a skinny, reddish-brown thing—lounged side by side with her fence lizard. "She's a four-toed salamander! I found her in the moss by the pond right next to that rotten log. The perfect ending to the perfect day!"

What would the perfect ending to my day have been? Getting tarred and feathered?

"Look! She's waving her tail. That means she's scared of you." Lizzy finger-stroked it.

"Feeling's mutual," I said, grossed out by the creepy toes.

Inside the house, Lizzy set dinner on the table while she told Dad and me all about sixth grade. She loved the teachers, the students, the school—everything. During dinner she talked so much Dad barely had time to quiz us. I got away with "fine," "uh-huh," "don't know yet," and "okay" until dessert.

"So, Winnie . . ." Dad twirled his fork, making lines in Lizzy's lemon pie. "Meet any kids with horses?"

I wished I could have told him I'd talked to even one kid about my horse business. But I hadn't even talked to one kid about anything.

"Towaco's really coming along well, Dad," I said, my stomach trying to shove the whole dinner back up.

"Uh-huh," Dad said, his lips twisting the way they do when he's disappointed.

The phone rang.

"I'll get it!" I scooted away from the table, never more saved by the bell. "Hello?"

"Lizzy?" came the voice at the other end. "Didn't it rock today when—?"

"This isn't Lizzy," I interrupted.

"Ohhh," said the disappointed caller.

"I'll get her."

The phone rang all evening, each call for Lizzy. I stopped answering after the third call. I couldn't stand disappointing anyone else.

The next day, Thursday, I woke up determined to give school another chance. I arrived on Lizzy-time and took a seat in Ms. Brumby's classroom.

Summer made her entrance, flanked by three girls who laughed at everything she said.

Hawk trailed them silently, with barely a glance at me.

"Honestly," Summer was saying to her adoring crowd, "if anyone ever saw me without makeup, I swear I'd transfer right out of this school!"

Note to self: Do everything within your power to see Summer Spidell without makeup.

Ms. Brumby led a discussion on the purpose of nursery rhymes as groundwork to our study of Shakespeare and the world's great poets. I was determined to make a comment. Twice I raised my hand, but she called on Grant. And he gave an answer that sounded 10 times as smart as mine would have.

We moved through the cat and the fiddle, the mouse up the clock, and the spider beside her.

Come on, Winnie. You have to say something. Time's running out.

"At last . . ." Ms. Brumby checked her gold watch that matched everything else she had on. "We come to 'Humpty Dumpty.'"

Kids picked up notebooks and backpacks, waiting for the buzzer.

"Now, class, don't disappoint me," coaxed Ms. Brumby. "'Humpty Dumpty sat on a wall. Humpty Dumpty had a great fall.' Anyone . . . ?"

Grant slipped on his backpack.

Now was my chance. I might not get another one. I raised my hand.

"Winifred?" Ms. Brumby's head moved slightly side to side, as if warming up for being shaken no.

I *had* to say something. "I think he was pushed!" I blurted.

A couple of kids laughed out loud.

Why did I say that? But now that I had, I had to back it up. "Yeah. Humpty Dumpty . . . he didn't fall. He was pushed! By all the king's men. And that part about the horses putting him back together? That's a cover-up, because how would horses do that?"

Summer giggled. Someone groaned.

Barker leaned over and whispered, "I thought that was good."

Ms. Brumby's face looked like she'd eaten a rotten hedge apple. "These rhymes have survived throughout the ages, class. We shouldn't waste valuable time making fun of them."

The buzzer rang, and I got out of there as fast as I could.

Pat's class was the only decent hour in the whole day. She brought up eternity again and got everybody trying to define *life*. Then she gave us an assignment to write a paper defining success in life.

Our math teacher gave out assignments like

he thought his was our only class. After math, red-haired Sal introduced me to none other than Grant . . . again. And again he showed no sign of recognizing me.

After school I watched Catman answer e-mails, typing twice as fast as I can. And he only used his thumbs and pinkies.

> Dear Catman,
> My cat fell off the back of my chair and broke her hip! I thought cats always landed on their feet. Is my cat stupid?
> —Feline2

Catman's answer came fast, with no mistakes:

> Peace, Feline2,
> No, man! Cats can't handle short falls. They dig long falls—more time to pull up the head, flip over, flatten, and use that tail for balance. Be careful with your feline, Cat!
> —The Catman

His last e-mail read:

> Hey, Catman!
> My kitty thinks she's an alarm clock! She pounces on me at five every A.M.

And she won't stop yowling until I get up and feed her. You gotta help! I fell asleep in school today!
—Kittykid

Far out, Kittykid!
You got yourself one smart kitty! She's trained you to feed her on command. Better stop feeding her at five. Praise her later when you do feed her. Tell your kitty to let sleeping cats lie!
—The Catman

I answered three quick questions about bridling a fussy horse, horse dieting, and giving a horse bath to a water-hating Tennessee Walker.

Pat read the screen. "Lands, I'd never come up with that in a month of Sundays! God was looking out for me the day you walked into this pet shop, Winnie!"

I bit the inside of my cheek. It felt good to have somebody think I did something right.

The bell announced a customer. Pat squinted toward the door, then strode to the front. "Well, will you lookie here what the cat dragged in, no offense! How's life treating you, Chubs?"

The tall, parent-aged man in gray slacks and a white shirt didn't look chubby. He grinned down at Pat. "Nobody's called me Chubs for a long time, Pat." They fell into easy conversation, and I went back to e-mails.

I'd almost finished when Pat put her hand on my shoulder. "This here's Winnie Willis! You're in luck, Chubs! Good horse gentlers are scarcer than hens' teeth, no offense!"

The man looked disappointed. "How old are you?"

"Twelve," I admitted, my voice cracking.

He cleared his throat, then shook his head like Ms. Brumby did when she expected me to say something stupid.

"Now, Chubs!" Pat chided. "Don't go looking a gift horse in the mouth! No offense. Winnie, this is Chubby Baines, a school chum of mine back in the Stone Age." Pat flicked a curl off her forehead. "He runs that store on Baney Road."

"*Chad* Baines," he corrected.

"I've been telling Chubs all about you," Pat explained.

"You have?" I glanced from one to the other.

"He's gotten himself into a real pickle, haven't you, Chubs?" Pat teased.

Chad Baines tugged his ear. "I bought a horse for my boy—good Quarter Horse gelding."

"He bought him off old Mrs. Reed," Pat interrupted. "Her husband and mine used to do business. Any-who, she had two horses. Chubs got one. Spider Spidell bought the other, a chestnut mare."

I nodded. So far I wasn't getting this.

"Spider's horse is no better than mine!" Mr. Baines insisted like I'd just said it was. "Although to hear Spider tell it, he got the bargain and I got the lemon."

"Can't I just hear the two of you going at it!" Pat exclaimed. "These boys competed over everything in school! Basketball, football, girls! And they haven't outgrown that nonsense, have you, Chubs?"

Mr. Baines's face flushed. "We got carried away. One thing led to another, and we ended up with a showdown. We gave ourselves one week to practice. Then his horse is going up against mine in a barrel race."

I cleared my own throat. "But you got a good horse, right?"

"I did!" Baines insisted. "Only the fool horse has gone downhill since we brought it home.

The more my son rides that gelding, the worse it gets. He can't even get his leads anymore. I hate to think I really did buy a lemon. A week from Saturday we go up against Spidell's little girl. If she wins, I'll never hear the end of it."

Pat chuckled. "Chubs couldn't exactly take the horse to Stable-Mart for training! So he dropped in on his old classmate for help. And I told him he needs to hire you!"

My heart sped up like a trotting horse in a harness race. *Hire me? Thank you, God!*

Mr. Baines handed me his business card. "I'll pay your monthly fee for just over a week's work if you can get this horse competition-ready."

My throat went dry. A month's pay! "Yeah!" I sounded like a stupid kid instead of a business-woman, but I didn't care. I had another client! Something good to tell Dad. I tried to focus on what Mr. Baines was saying.

"Then I'll bring him over to your place tonight, if that's all right."

"Tonight?" My brain tried to rein in the infor-mation.

"Good." He nodded, and Pat escorted him to the door.

Barker came over, holding three white puppies that reminded me of Lizzy's old battery toy dog that barked and turned back flips. "Way to go, Winnie! Are Quarter Horses hard to train?"

"Not usually. And they're naturally fast— fastest horse for the quarter mile. So the speed should be there for the barrel race."

"Especially if the horse just races barrels." Catman had sneaked up on us.

"Funny, Catman." I gave him my crooked grin. "Haven't you guys seen horses race a cloverleaf pattern around three barrels? Best time wins."

I wasn't crazy about barrel racing or any racing. God built horses to run all out only when they're frightened, the flee response. Making them compete forces horses to strain.

"So when's the dude delivering the horse?" Catman asked.

When is he delivering the horse? I tried to replay what Mr. Baines said. *Tonight?*

"Tonight!" I screamed, toppling the computer chair as I jerked up. "I have to get home! The stall, the barn. The yard! Dad's mess!"

Barker wanted to help, but his parents were

picking him up to help move Great-granny Barker in with them. That meant Lizzy would be babysitting.

I yelled thanks to Pat and started home.

Catman followed me without a word. The sun hung low in the sky as we walked our bikes over the unmown grass through our littered yard.

"Found it!" Dad bounced up from a pile of metal. He held up a piece of coated wiring. "Catman! For the back-bike horn!"

"Cool!" Catman ogled the stupid wire.

I stepped over tires, small appliances, and machine guts to reach the rusted-out washing machine Dad called his worktable. "Dad, I got a new client!"

"That's great, Winnie!" Dad twisted the wire into a funnel that already had enough wires sticking out of it to light up Ashland.

"Try this." Catman handed Dad a paper clip.

"A paying customer!" I continued.

"Good for you!" Dad dropped to all fours and felt in the grass. "Another horse?"

No, an elephant. Winnie the Elephant Gentler.

I paced the yard, kicking spokes, pipes, and all

kickable junk out of my way. I dumped toasters, grills, and other "works-in-progress" behind the house.

"Got it!" Catman held up the funnel, now attached to a tiny black box. He pressed a button, and out came *meow! MEOW!*

"Meow?" I imagined biking backwards while meowing.

"Churchill's voice," Catman explained.

Dad looked as if he'd just invented the Internet. "But it could say *woof* or *neigh* or *oink . . ."*

Which are so much less embarrassing.

I gave up on the yard and headed for the barn. Nickers gave me a warm nicker. I nuzzled her long enough to calm down and shoot up a prayer. *Thanks for Nickers. And thanks for the new client. You know how much I want to impress Mr. Baines and his son. Could you show me how I should act around them?*

Catman came in, four cats at his heels. "They're here. I'm off." He flashed me the hang loose sign.

I raced to the yard in time to see a cream-colored trailer ease to a stop. Dad was gone. Mr. Baines climbed out of the cab. "My son here yet? He was supposed to meet me here after football practice."

"I haven't seen anybody," I said.

The trailer rocked. The horse was restless, eager to get out. He kicked the sides. *Bang! Bang!*

"That animal! I thought we'd never get him in there." Mr. Baines backhanded sweat from his forehead. "Can't say I'm looking forward to getting him out." He squinted down our road. "Where *is* that boy? I told him I needed him here!"

"Can I unload your horse?" I moved toward the tailgate.

"Be my guest." He let down the tail ramp and stood back.

"Easy, fella." I stepped into a nice, two-horse trailer and moved up the empty side. "Good horse."

"You wouldn't say that if you'd seen him load," Mr. Baines muttered.

My eyes adjusted to the darkness of the trailer, and I saw by the horse's rump that he was a deep bay with great conformation. His coal black tail, coarser than Nickers', looked healthy.

Inching my way toward his head, I touched

his back. His skin twitched, setting off his legs in shifts, like running in place.

"You can't wait to get out, can you, big guy?" Something about the horse looked or smelled familiar. I moved up the withers to his neck and his close-cropped, black mane.

I heard a car drive up. Someone got out and slammed the door too hard. The car drove off.

"You're okay," I told the gelding. By the time I reached his neck, I knew I'd seen this horse before.

He craned his head around to see me. In the middle of his forehead was a white star.

"You! Star?" That was the name I'd given the horse that awful morning in the field, seconds before my backward ride. Eager Star! "But you can't be!" I whispered. "'Cause if you're Eager Star, then that means—"

Footsteps sounded behind the trailer. "Sorry I'm late, Dad."

That golden-toned voice, that perfect pronunciation . . . *Grant!*

$\mathcal{I}$ wanted to stay inside the trailer with Eager Star. Grant! Head-of-the-herd Grant! I'd signed on to gentle Grant's horse? He'd never let it happen. He'd seen me riding backwards! What would his dad say when he found out that little piece of information? Besides, Grant would never agree to let the mousy new girl train his horse.

Star strained at his leadrope.

"Easy." I untied him. Outside the trailer, Grant and his dad were arguing. I tuned them out. "Remember me, Star?" Gently I blew into his nostrils, an old Navajo practice my mom taught me. Greet a horse the way they greet one another. If they blow back, you've got a friend.

Eager Star nodded, then snorted back. At least I had one Baines on my side.

Naming a horse had been a big deal to Mom and me in Wyoming. Neither of us liked to give a horse an actual name unless we knew we'd be keeping it. Too hard to let go. But since I'd needed to call the horse something that day I met him, I'd made up a temporary name. And Eager Star had come by his name before I'd ever dreamed of working with him.

"Time to face the humans," I whispered. "Back."

The bay responded to my voice command and stepped backward, too fast, but steady all the way down the ramp.

Outside, the sunset left enough light for me to glimpse Grant and his dad still arguing. Keeping the horse between me and them, I hollered, "I'll just take him to the barn!"

Mr. Baines stopped shouting. I braced myself. He strode to my side of the horse and yelled, "Grant, get over here!"

My stomach knotted, and my ears buzzed. I stared at my boots and tried to predict whether Grant would act disgusted or laugh outright the minute he saw me. I wanted this job. We needed this job.

"Grant," his father barked, "this is the girl who's going to try to fix whatever you did to this horse."

Biting my lip, I glanced up, ready for the worst.

"Glad to meet you," Grant mumbled. I thought I saw a flicker of recognition, but it went out quickly. He looked through me, just like at school.

Unbelievable! He really doesn't recognize me.

"Dad, you want me to take Bad Boy now?" Grant sounded strained, anxious, not like school Grant. "I could settle him down before we go."

Mr. Baines made a sound that would have been a snort in a horse. "Yeah, right. You *can't* settle him down. Remember? That's why we're here." He waved his hand as if he were shooing flies. "Stay, go. I don't care." He stormed toward the trailer.

Eager Star danced sideways, anxious to get going. I willed Grant to leave with his dad. But he followed me to the barn. "So what are my chances of winning?"

I shrugged. "I won't know 'til I work with

your horse." The bay edged ahead of me, and I circled him.

Grant scurried out of the way. "If Bad Boy doesn't win, I—"

"Bad Boy?" I interrupted.

"Baines's Bad Boy. That's his name."

We entered the barn.

"It's a lousy name."

Grant shrugged. "I haven't thought about it."

Star's nostrils flared as he took in the barn smell of horses and hay. That's when I noticed the tiny scrapes at his muzzle. Anger surged through me like electricity. "Did you load this horse into the trailer?"

"What?" Grant seemed distracted. "Uh, no. I had practice."

I scratched the bay's neck, and he stretched it out, shoving his nose in my face. The scrapes had come from a twitch, a device some horsemen use to make a horse go where it doesn't want to go. A rope noose loops around the upper lip. The loop is attached to what looks like a bat, and the bat is twisted, tightening the noose around the horse's muzzle until he gives in. Mr. Baines had done that to Grant's horse.

I was so close to telling Grant off, the words burned in my throat. The Baineses obviously believed in punishment training. Mom had taught me there were two kinds of horse trainers—punishers and gentlers. Lots of horse trainers believe the only way to teach a horse is to punish him when he steps out of line. Mom believed in praising a horse for the things he does right.

I stroked the star on the gelding's forehead, pure white against his dark brown face. "I'll be calling this horse Eager Star."

Grant moved in beside me and stroked the star too. He towered over me, a full head taller. "Eager Star. I like it."

Nickers came in from the pasture.

"Company, Nickers!" I led Star over to Nickers. "Meet Eager Star."

Nickers nodded, her silky mane stirring like angel wings.

"Is that your—?" Grant stopped and stared at Nickers. "Wait a minute! That's what I've been trying to think of!" He wheeled around to face me. "I've seen that white horse before—in the field!"

Great! Nickers, he remembers. Me? I might as well have been a blade of grass.

"And you . . . you're *her!* You're the girl who rides backward!"

Okay. I'd rather be grass.

My mind shot me a photo of Grant tearing out after the other rider. "Well, I wouldn't have been riding backward if you and Brian hadn't taken off in some stupid race!"

Grant slapped his forehead. "You're Pat's Pet! And the Humpty Dumpty detective! 'He was pushed!'" He burst out laughing.

My breath came in ragged spurts as I led Star to his stall. My heart pounded in my ears. "Nice to know I'm not totally invisible!" I stormed to the grain bin, afraid of what else I might say. *Okay, God,* I prayed as I dipped up a scoopful of oats. *I could bite like a Mustang. Don't let me go off on Grant.*

By the time I finished graining the horses, I'd at least given up the notion of biting.

Grant had stopped laughing. "Sorry. Really. That day in the field, I should have come back to see if you were okay. It's just—I didn't want to lose to Brian and—"

"No, you wouldn't want to lose." Lizzy would have hated the edge in my voice. Mom too.

"I'm sorry, okay? And that Humpty Dumpty

stuff was great—the only laugh we've had in Brumby's boring class."

I would have guessed he loved Brumby and English. "It *is* pretty boring, isn't it?" I risked a glance at him, and he grinned.

"Which reminds me, I have homework! I missed one on Haven's quiz. I should have memorized her notes." He walked toward the barn door.

I followed him. "You mean that stuff about life goals and how long you expect to live and stuff?" *Smooth, Winnie! Can you say* stuff *one more time?* "I don't think she's going to grade that stuff." *Great! You* can *say* stuff *one more time.*

"Never know." We stepped outside. We'd been in the barn long enough that the night had grown black except for a handful of stars. "Besides," Grant continued, "it's her first impression of us. Life science is a big class for me. I might want to become a surgeon. I should have studied more."

I shook my head. Grant Baines was about as opposite from Catman Coolidge as you can get. Dr. Baines, the surgeon, and Catman Coolidge, the telegraph operator.

I walked him through the yard, and he kept

going. Then he turned back. In the dark, he looked like a shadow. "Bye, Winnie. See you tomorrow!"

See invisible me tomorrow? Wouldn't that be something!

Chapter

9

$\mathcal{F}$riday morning I left home later than planned. I'd ridden Nickers at dawn, fed Towaco and Eager Star, and mucked the barn before getting dressed for school. But what slowed me down was writing in my private journal after breakfast:

Herd behavior in kids at AMS makes it almost impossible for a new person to break in. Still, individual members of the popular herd may act different when they're away from the pack. Take Grant, the head stallion of the popular group. Last night he almost acted like a regular guy. If Summer or Brian had been here, I doubt if Grant would have wasted his time on a straggling scrub like me.

I wheeled my bike into the rack, then spotted Summer and Grant's herd on the steps, blocking traffic so kids had to squeeze around them to get inside.

Great! I'd have to walk right by the herd. What if Grant had already told everybody about my backward ride on Nickers? Summer would love that!

Laughter erupted from their group, no doubt at my expense.

I climbed the steps, pretending not to see or hear them. *See no evil. Hear no ev–*

"Winnie!" Grant shouted.

I glanced behind me, as if there might be another Winnie on the steps.

"Come here!" Grant motioned me into the herd.

Swallowing what felt like sandpaper, I joined them, wishing I'd spent more than two seconds on my hair. I wore jeans; they wore shorts. I needed a new top so I wouldn't have to repeat in the same week. Summer probably didn't repeat her clothes the whole year.

"How's Towaco?" Hawk moved over so I could stand next to her.

"He's good." *Loosen up, Winnie girl! Just a herd of horses. You like horses.*

Hawk's shorts matched her peacock shirt. "Grant told us you are training his horse."

I looked at Grant, amazed. He'd told them

that? He hadn't told them about the backward ride? "Uh-huh." *Great conversation, Winnie. You really belong in this herd.*

Summer laughed. She looked to the other members of the herd, the real members. "Grant and I have to race in a barrel race our dads dreamed up. Not like I want to! I don't even like riding Western. Daddy's making me practice, practice, practice! He's driving me crazy!"

That's a short putt.

Grant cracked his knuckles.

"So, Summer . . ." Sal reached back to redo her red ponytail. "How's it coming with the sleepover plans?"

"My mother ordered in so much food! We'll gain 10 pounds!" Summer tugged at the tiny black belt at her waist.

"Bet you wish *you* were coming tonight, Grant!" cooed a girl with pixie short, blonde hair. I didn't recognize her from any of my classes. I *knew* she didn't recognize me.

"I'll pass." Grant still flashed his perfect smile, but it looked forced—all lips, no eyes.

Hawk secretly elbowed me. "Summer, have you invited Winnie yet?"

I elbowed Hawk back. I was kind of surprised

she'd say it, because Summer Spidell would sooner invite the plague or pimples than me.

Startled, Summer looked at Grant, who simply stared back as if waiting for the answer.

"From what I hear," Grant said, "girls go to Summer's parties so they won't get gossiped about. Better go, Winnie."

Me? At the popular girls' party? Some of the girls have horses. I could talk about horse gentling. . . . Then I came to my senses. No way would Summer make me part of her herd!

I shrugged.

Summer giggled in a girlish way I couldn't have pulled off if I took classes in it. "Grant Baines!" She sent a fake smile in my general direction without taking her eyes off Grant. "Of course you'll come, Winnie!"

Hawk elbowed me. "Great! We'll go together."

I could feel the sappy grin on my face. But I couldn't do anything about it. The last time I'd been invited to a sleepover, I still wore cowboy pj's and slept with a stuffed horse. And now here I was, partying with the popular herd! It had all happened just like with horses in the wild. I'd made friends with the herd leader, and

I'd been accepted into the herd. Lizzy would freak! Even Dad would be impressed.

Grant glanced at his watch. "I've gotta go over my notes before class. See you."

His loyal herd watched as he trotted up the steps. The blonde and two girls I'd seen in the cafeteria headed inside, too, leaving Sal, Summer, Hawk, and me.

The minute Grant disappeared into the building, Summer snapped her fingers and turned to me. "Oh no!" She tilted her head to the side and stuck out pouty lips. "I forgot. My mother laid down the law. I can't invite more than nine girls. And I've already invited . . . let me see here . . ." She counted on her fingers. ". . . nine. Sorry, Winifred. By the way, I was so relieved *you*'d be training Grant's horse. I hate to lose."

She started to go, then laughed and called back, "Hey! Speaking of *losing*, don't *lose* Grant's horse!"

I should have known. Nothing—not even Grant— could make Summer invite me!

"But you said—," Hawk started.

"Forget it!" I snapped, mad at myself for getting sucked in. Summer and I are two different breeds. Summer would never feel what I was feeling, the kick in the stomach when you're thrown out of the herd. Never. She got invited to everything.

Just once I wish *she'd* feel left out. I wish *she* could be the one not invited. I should have thrown a party and not invited her! "I'm too busy anyway."

"I suppose you are!" Summer agreed. "You must have tons to do just to get up to speed on barrel racing."

That does it! I'm sick of letting her make me feel bad! Well it's her turn, just this once, to feel bad.

I managed a sugary smile. "The race . . . and my overnight deal." I glanced at my watch, just the right touch of disinterest.

Hawk didn't miss a beat. "You're right, Winnie! I can't believe how much we still have to do! And only a week away!" Hawk was good. She was really coming through for me. Giving it a real date made the whole thing sound more real.

Sal looked hurt. "Hey, I'm the one who said your memory's tight! What's with not inviting me?"

"Of course you're invited, Sal," Hawk said.

Wait a minute. There's nothing to invite her to.

"Good!" Sal grinned. "My little brother is in your sister's class. She brought in cookies he won't stop talking about. Is she baking for your party?"

Party? This has gone far enough. Say something, Winnie!

"You can't invite Sal and not invite me," Summer whined.

Ha! There it is, what I wanted—Summer feeling left out. Time to admit it was just a joke. "Come on, Winnie," Hawk urged.

Summer gave me her puppy-dog look. Where was Barker, the dog expert, when I needed him?

"Summer . . ." I looked at her—the perfect clothes and perfect hair. How could I tell her I had nothing going on, no party, nothing? "Sure."

The bell rang, and Sal and Summer ran in. Hawk and I trailed after them.

"Did we just invite them to my house?" I asked, feeling sick to my stomach. I should have known not to try to get even. Lizzy's told me a hundred times that revenge is God's department, not mine. "Hawk, what am I going to do now?"

"You are going to have the most popular girls

in seventh over!" Hawk whispered. "I can help you."

"Help me what? Get a new house?"

I got to English just as Ms. Brumby was shutting the door.

Sliding into my seat, I made a mental list: clean house, ask Lizzy to plan food, move to Siberia.

While Grant and Ms. Brumby kept up a discussion on "The Raven," I pulled out my personal journal and wrote:

Old mares dominate a pack, much like English teachers rule classrooms. These old mares were probably rejected from herds when they were young.

A shadow passed over my notebook, and I closed it fast. Ms. Brumby stood in front of my desk and stared down at my journal. When she didn't speak, I smiled up at her, hoping she wouldn't ask me a question about what they'd been discussing. I didn't have a clue.

But instead of tricking me with a question or yelling at me for not paying attention, she thanked me. "Thank you, Winifred. I nearly forgot. Class, pass your journals to the end of your row."

I was so relieved, I dropped my pen.

Barker plopped half a dozen notebooks on my desk. I tossed mine to the bottom of the pile and passed them on. Close call!

I couldn't wait for school to end so I could get in a great first workout with Eager Star. I answered six e-mails at Pat's Pets, then raced home and told Lizzy about what I'd gotten myself into.

"Winnie! Sweet! I'll make pizza and brownies! And isn't God just the greatest! *Thanks, God, for giving Winnie friends already!* And sprinkles on the brownies!" She prayed so much like Mom it hurt.

Walking to the pasture I prayed, *Sorry it took me this long to say thanks, God. So thanks. It would be a miracle if we really pulled this party thing off. And if you let Star win that race, well, I'd like that a lot. That's all.*

Nickers greeted me in the paddock. I put my

cheek against hers and inhaled her earthy horse smell as if she were oxygen. "Can't ride you now. Got to get Star in championship shape."

Towaco galloped up, and Nickers shot back her ears. But it was a bluff. The two horses had been getting along.

Eager Star let me catch him and lead him in to be tacked up. Usually I ride bareback. I love being close enough to the horse to sense what he's feeling before he moves on it. But Grant would be racing Summer in Western tack. So that's how I'd train him. Every practice had to count.

I led Star to the cross-ties, two straps coming from opposite walls of the stallway. They hook onto a horse's halter for easier grooming. Star stood for me as I reached for the cross-ties. But the minute I hooked his halter, he snorted and pulled back.

"Easy!"

But he backed up, jerking his head against the ties.

"Whoa!" I reached up and tried to unhook him, wishing I weren't so short. Finally, I got it. "What's wrong with you? You can't be this nervous, Star!"

Untied, Star stood still while I saddled him. But in the paddock, it took me three tries to mount because he wouldn't stand still. I laid the reins on Star's neck. He lunged as if he'd been snakebit.

Star responded to voice cues, trotting when I called, "Trot." But his wild trot threatened to break into a canter. I had to pull on his reins more than I liked. Instead of walking like an easygoing Quarter Horse, he pranced like an American Saddlebred. I couldn't get his gallop down to a canter, much less to the lope I was going for. I had to correct him at every step.

"You *have* to get your leads," I pleaded.

In a canter, horses reach farther forward with the front and hind legs on one side—left legs in a left lead when cantering counterclockwise, right when going clockwise. Wrong leads make bumpy rides. A cutting horse can't even get around a barrel if he throws the wrong lead.

I worked Star until dark. He missed more leads than he got.

As I cooled him down, I had to wonder if Spider Spidell was right. Maybe Mr. Baines did buy a lemon.

I felt bad for Eager Star. If I couldn't get him

ready for that race, Mr. Baines would sell him. I felt just as bad for me. Summer and her dad wouldn't let any of us forget my failure. What if nobody ever trusted me as a horse gentler again?

I'd promised Barker I'd come over so we could work together on our papers for Pat's class. I scarfed down Lizzy's chili for supper and was about to take off when the phone rang.

Dad got it and held the receiver away from his ear. I recognized the blustery voice on the other end: "Sa-a-ay!"

Catman's dad was calling about the business lunch!

"Well, I don't know," Dad said. "Next Saturday?" He looked at Lizzy and me as if we'd throw him a lifeline.

I nodded. "Do it, Dad! Go! You'll make lots of contacts."

He squinted at me. "I guess . . . thanks." He hung up, not sounding like he meant thanks.

I explained to Lizzy. "Dad's going to the Ashland business luncheon!" It felt like our first break since Chubs Baines walked into Pat's Pets. "Catman's dad says it's the first step in getting a good business reputation in Ashland."

Dad rubbed the stubble on his chin. "Thought I'd left business meetings in Laramie. I've met a couple of those men—I don't mean Mr. Coolidge. But I wonder if I fit in anymore."

Barker waved from the porch swing of a two-story house that looked fixed-up old. White-gold light streamed through the long windows, along with shouts and laughter. Macho, their black-and-tan dog, sat at Barker's feet, next to Chico, the white Chihuahua. Barker whistled, and the sweetest collie trotted out of the bushes. "Have you met Underdog?"

The collie thumped its tail when I petted it. Barker took dogs everyone else had given up on and trained them for his five brothers.

"Sorry I'm late." I sat next to him on the swing. "Lousy first workout. I don't know if I can get Grant's horse in shape for the race or not."

Somebody shouted from inside. "Come on in now!"

I didn't know if they meant us or the dogs, but Chico took it as an order. He darted to the door, toenails clicking across the porch.

Barker jumped up. "No, Chico!"

He was too late. Chico rammed the screen. He shook his head and ran at it again.

Barker snatched up the pup. "When are you going to believe me, Chico? You can't go through doors."

The Barker home smelled like real food, maybe a roast. Two of Barker's brothers chased past us and up the stairs. Mark and Luke are only a year apart, but Luke is small for his age, kind of like his dog, Chico. Mark, age seven, is the athletic one, his arms already showing muscles from throwing his Lab the Frisbee night and day.

On an overstuffed sofa an old woman sat with a big, plastic bowl on her lap. She had pure white hair that looked like she'd just finished a high-speed chase in a top-down convertible. The arms that stuck out of her flowered dress were stick thin. She smiled with eyes that looked like they'd seen angels.

"Granny, this is Winnie, a friend of mine." Barker shouted, but the woman didn't seem to hear . . . or understand. "Winnie, this is my great-grandmother . . . Granny for short. We've got homework, Granny," Barker explained.

Granny kept snapping the fresh beans in her bowl into smaller pieces and staring out the window as if it were a TV. I liked that Barker didn't feel he had to explain her.

He set his notebook on a nearby table. "Here's where I study."

Barker's mother brought in lemonade and chips. "Good to see you, Winnie!"

I'd met her a couple of times when she'd picked up Lizzy for church. Mrs. Barker taught computer science, but she could have been a model. She was tall, with wavy hair, brown eyes, deep brown skin. "Eddy's dad is teaching a night poetry class. He'll be sorry he missed you." She turned to Eddy's great-grandmother. "Granny? More lemonade?"

Great-granny Barker's only answer was the steady *snap, snap, snap* of the beans.

"Where Wizzy?" asked William, who had just started talking. His face was round as a cookie, and his hair stuck out longer than the other boys' hair.

His brothers filed in behind him.

"Yeah, where's Lizzy?" Matthew, at nine, was the only Barker who didn't smile much. He had his bulldog on a leash. Their frowns matched.

Mrs. Barker snatched up the two younger boys. "Winnie and Eddy have to study. Besides, you guys need baths!" She made a face that cracked up four out of the five. "And I'll read an extra Bible story to the one who gets the cleanest."

They thundered upstairs, leaving Granny snapping beans while Barker and I talked about our papers.

Every idea I could think of for defining success in life sounded too stupid in my head for me to let it out of my mouth. "Right now success would be getting Eager Star to win the barrel race. But I don't think that's enough to write about."

"Enough what?" Mrs. Barker, her arms full of clothes, swept past us, then slid into the empty chair at our table.

Barker explained our assignment. Then his mom leaned forward. "What do you really want, Winnie?"

I want Star to beat Summer's horse. I want Grant and his dad to be super impressed. I want the kids at school to be impressed. I want Dad to be impressed.

I shrugged.

Mrs. Barker wouldn't let me off. "What would success be for Winnie Willis?"

"I want to be known as the best horse gentler in the world," I said, trying to make it sound like a joke.

Barker's mom smiled. "How about you, Eddy?" She turned his notebook so she could read what he'd written: "Colossians 3:23."

"What's it say?" I asked. Lizzy and Mom would have known.

Barker said it from memory: "'Work hard and cheerfully at whatever you do, as though you were working for the Lord rather than for people.'"

I knew it wasn't something Barker wrote to sound good. He worked hard and was happy. He probably did work for God. I tried to imagine what it would feel like to work for God instead of Mr. Baines.

"I know God would make a great boss and everything . . ." I was thinking out loud, but Barker and his mom didn't make me feel stupid. "Only knowing me, I'd probably still want to win the barrel race to impress God just like I want to impress Mr. Baines." *And Grant. And Summer. And Dad . . .*

The *snaps* stopped, and from the couch came a throaty noise.

We turned to Great-granny Barker.

"Child," she said, not taking her gaze from the window, "God ain't waiting at no finish line. No, Jesus is running with you, caring more about the steps on the way than the big finish. Can't nobody impress God. Just look at what he created out there!"

Outside her window, a blanket of lightning bugs blinked on and off below while above, the whole sky blinked stars.

"You're right, Ma!" Mrs. Barker wiped her eyes.

I didn't want to forget what she'd said even though I didn't really understand what it meant. *He cares more about the steps than the finish?* I reached into my backpack and pulled out my notebook, flipping pages until I got to a blank one.

"Winnie?" Barker reached for my notebook and turned to the cover. "Didn't you turn in your journal to Ms. Brumby?"

"Yeah." I glanced at the notebook in front of me. "I turned in my class journal. This one is my personal—" I stopped, the words cut off, along with my oxygen. "But this should be gray—" I stared at the cover of the journal, the *red* journal, my classroom journal for Ms. Brumby. "This can't be red!"

I dumped out my backpack. No gray journal. Dizzy, I yanked my notebook off the table and stared at the cover again, as if it might magically change from red to gray.

"It's not possible," I muttered, gripping the notebook so tight a page ripped. "I know I turned in my journal." I remembered adding mine to the bottom of the stack before passing it on. "But if this is my class journal, then that means—" I couldn't finish. I stood up so suddenly my chair fell backward. "I'm sorry. I have to go." My heart pounded like horses galloping. Horses! I tried to remember everything I'd written in the gray journal about the Ashland Middle School herd, the comments about the mares and stallions. The "Old Mare Teacher!"

Every word I'd written for my eyes only was now in the hands of Barb Brumby.

115

$\mathcal{S}$he won't read it, I told myself as I pedaled backwards in the dark. Ms. Brumby's too busy to read journals. She just wants to make sure we've written something. Anything. Maybe I'll get a great grade for writing so much.

By the time I reached home, I'd almost convinced myself.

Until I saw Dad.

He was sitting in his reading chair, his back to the door. Slowly, he folded the paper, took off his glasses, and turned to face me. "You know, I wish just once I could go an entire semester without hearing, 'Mr. Willis, I'm calling about your daughter Winifred.'"

I tried to explain about the two journals getting mixed up. "And besides, it wasn't really my fault. Remember? Picturing people as horses was really your idea in the first place."

"True enough," Dad said. "But that's not the problem, Winnie. Most of what you wrote sounded . . . well, creative. Ms. Brumby liked several of your comparisons between students and horses. Except some of the things about the *lead mare?*"

"It's not fair, Dad! You don't know Ms. Brumby. She's cold and mean, and she hates me!"

"Winnie, that's enough," he said quietly, which worried me more than if he'd just yelled and gotten it over with. "I had a long talk with Ms. Brumby. She's a caring teacher who only wants what's best for you. She's concerned that you feel alienated in your new school. And, quite frankly, so am I. She sees you connecting everything to horses, but not relating to your peers. If you could have heard the concern in her voice, Winnie!"

They clone them! Every rotten teacher I'd ever had turned out some caring imitation whenever parents were around.

Dad went on for a few minutes about starting fresh and giving Ms. Brumby and the other kids a chance. I sat tight-lipped, wondering what it would feel like to have Dad talk to me this long when he wasn't angry. For some reason, whenever Dad and I were together, we both missed Mom so much we couldn't stand it.

When I got up to leave, I couldn't help but think, *Mom would have listened to my side about the journals. She would have understood.*

By the time I went to bed, Lizzy was asleep, and I had to trip over my floor junk. I said my prayers and asked God to bless everybody. Then I added, *And please don't let me disappoint Dad again.*

Saturday I woke with a queasy stomach. *Get ready, Star. You have one week to become the greatest barrel racer this side of Texas! We can't disappoint Grant or his dad . . . or mine.*

"Going to rain," Lizzy announced when I came outside. She wiped her forehead with a hand that had been digging in dirt.

I glanced at the cloudless sky and had to squint at the sun. "You're crazy, Lizzy!"

She pulled three gross worms out of the ground. "I hear that?"

I listened. Towaco whinnied. Beach Boys music blared from Dad's bedroom. "What?"

"Frogs going crazy. Birds are quiet. Cows are lying down. Going to rain." Lizzy's voice was matter-of-fact.

Now I heard the steady croaking from the pond. I knew I should believe Lizzy. She can tell the temperature by how fast crickets chirp. But I couldn't find a single cloud in the sky. "Frogs are just in a good mood!" I called, jogging to the barn.

I'd no sooner hooked one cross-tie to Star's halter than he jerked back so hard the strap pulled out of the wall.

"Star!" I grabbed the strap before it could slap him.

He didn't run away but stood trembling, the broken strap dangling from his halter.

I sighed and unhooked the strap. "Eager Star, you want to tell me how a Quarter Horse gets this nervous?" A truly nervous horse is one of the few lost causes.

"Who you rapping with?" Catman had sneaked up like a cat burglar. He wore a purple shirt with a peace sign on it, denim bell-bottoms, and sandals.

"Catman, if I don't turn Grant's nervous horse into a champion barrel racer by next Saturday, nobody's ever going to come to Winnie the horse gentler again!"

Catman peered past me. "No barrels?"

"That's just one of my problems. Mr. Baines had said he'd drop off barrels. Spidells might even agree to have the race here. But so far, no barrels."

"Chill, Winnie." Catman shuffled away.

I had Star saddled when Catman returned with Barker and Lizzy. Giving them a quick wave, I made a moving mount and settled into the Western saddle. I wasn't so sure I wanted an audience.

"I don't know how I let Catman talk me into this!" Lizzy shouted as the three of them joined Star and me in the pasture.

"Personally," Barker said, "I've always wanted to be a barrel."

"Be a what?" I asked as I stared at them.

"Three, right?" Catman, for once, had to squint up at *me* as Star danced in place. Then he burst into song and a skip-shuffle that might have been the polka. "Roll out the barrels! We'll have a barrel of fun!"

He grabbed Lizzy and spun her to the far end of the paddock. Still singing, he polka-ed Barker to make the third point of his triangle.

When I stopped laughing, I went back to struggling with Star while they measured their positions—Catman and Barker 90 feet apart, 105 feet from Lizzy.

Lizzy wasn't laughing. "Winnie, that monster won't run over me, will it? You can control it?"

"Of course!" I shouted, wondering if I could. A few clouds chugged through the sky, and a breeze kicked up as I forced Star to the starting line. "I'll circle Barker, then Catman, then all out to Lizzy. Right, right, left. Slow and easy."

But Star strained at the bit and lunged before I could settle him at the starting line. Uncollected, he stumbled, then had to trot before breaking into a canter. We came at Barker in a wide-angled arc. I leaned to the right, but he overdid it and stumbled again. We circled Barker in a wide trot.

"Come on!" I urged Star to change leads. He didn't, and we bumped Catman, almost toppling him. On we ran straight toward Lizzy, picking up speed. Thunder clapped.

Lizzy screamed. She ran to the fence. "I can't be a barrel! Sorry!"

It didn't matter. The whole trial was a disaster. The sky opened, and down came the rain in sheets. Rumbling thunder shook the earth, and I knew the rain would last all day.

Catman and Barker hung out with me in the barn. I filled them in on the Brumby disaster. "Dad's making me write an apology letter to Ms. Brumby for calling her an old mare. Plus, I've still got Pat's assignment." I turned back to Barker. "Wish your great-grandmother could write my paper."

"What's happening with Ma Barker?" Catman asked. "The Colonel asks about her all the time. He digs her!"

Barker laughed. "Colonel Coolidge, Catman's great-grandpa. He's . . . well . . . unusual."

As opposed to the rest of the normal Coolidges? I made a mental note to steer clear of the colonel.

"Time to split." Catman headed out, with Barker close behind.

Then Barker yelled back, "Winnie, tell Lizzy we'll pick her up for church at nine!"

Back in Wyoming, Mom had made sure our

whole family went to church every Sunday. So far in Ohio, only Lizzy had gone. I missed it.

"Catman and I are coming too!" I hollered.

"The Colonel already told Bart and Claire and me we're 'cancelling any reservations to heaven' by having plastic Santa lawn decorations at Christmas."

"Doesn't work that way, Catman," Barker said. "Hey! Guess who's acting pastor tomorrow. Ralph Evans, from the animal shelter!"

Catman chuckled. "Ralph's acting like a pastor?"

Barker laughed. "Until we get someone full-time."

"Far out! This I gotta see!"

It was still raining Sunday when the Barkers drove up in their bright yellow van that should be a school bus. I was losing another day's train-ing, and time was running out.

Lizzy and I dashed out and slid into the middle seats. Granny and Mrs. Barker sat in front with Luke. I fastened my seat belt and fingered the little belts attached to the floor.

"Dog belts, Winnie," Mr. Barker explained from the backseat. "Your dad's invention."

I didn't know whether to be proud or embarrassed.

The small church with a real steeple looked cut out of a Christmas card. Barkers took up a whole pew, with me on the end. A dozen people greeted Lizzy. Pat waved across the aisle, and Catman strolled in just as the music started. He slid in so close we couldn't fit a hymnal between us.

"You clean up pretty good," Catman whispered, straightening his red tie, which was worn with a red T-shirt and red jeans. He shouted down the row as the organist pounded out "Amazing Grace," "Cool tunes, Lizzy!"

"Told you!" Lizzy whispered back.

Then Catman must have spotted Granny at the end of the pew. "Ma Barker! The Colonel sends his love!"

Granny kept staring straight ahead.

"She digs him," Catman whispered.

Nobody told us to pipe down. From the minute Ralph stood up, in khaki pants and tennis shoes, I felt like I'd been coming to this church my whole life. "Ever wonder what *praise* is?" he asked. "My granddaddy used to say, 'Praise and punishment. Them's the only two choices.'" It was what Mom always said about horse training.

Catman leaned over and whispered, "Here we go!"

But Ralph smiled right at Catman. "Punishment? Jesus took care of that by dying for us. So if you've taken that gift, then I reckon that leaves praise. God, good job on that rain! And the fresh smell of your pine trees. And colors! Like the light streaming through your stained-glass windows!"

His whole sermon, if you can call it that, was about giving and getting praise. I listened to every word and even looked up the verses in the pew Bible. But the phrase that knocked me over every time he said it was "All God's creatures need praise!"

It wasn't until the drive home that it all clicked in. *Praise!* I hadn't been punishing Star. But I hadn't praised him much either. I wanted to win that race so much, I'd forgotten one of Mom's main rules: You can always find something to praise the horse for. I'd been so down on Eager Star, I'd even thought he might be a lemon, a lost cause. He probably sensed that's how I felt.

I couldn't wait to start over with him.

It rained all day Sunday, but I hung out with the horses and told them how amazing they were. Monday, Labor Day, I was in the barn when the sun came up. *Help me find things to praise Star for,* I prayed as I called the bay in from the pasture. *And great job on this sunrise!*

I skipped the cross-ties and noticed something. Star always stood still with a dropped rein.

"Such a smart horse!" I told him.

His bridle had a high curbed bit, too punishing for my tastes. The bigger the curve in the metal, the harder it is on the horse's mouth. I switched to a snaffle, a broken bit that wouldn't hurt so much when the rider pulled back on the reins.

Mom taught me to guide horses with my legs and back, to give cues instead of using force to move a horse. I barely used the reins now as we trotted around the pasture.

Star tossed his head and didn't want to walk, but I noticed something else. He hardly sweated, even though the afternoon got hot. Nervous horses lather up a sweat even in cold weather, but not Eager Star.

"You're not nervous, are you, boy? Just eager to please." I'd seen it when I first met the bay and Grant in the fields and called the horse Eager Star.

That practice changed everything. Star still broke leads and tried to spurt ahead of me. But when Catman and Barker dropped by, this time with Hawk as the third barrel, it was a whole different scene. I let Star take the barrels at a trot in the opposite direction because I noticed he favored the left lead. I praised the bay at every turn. And my "barrels" cheered as we rounded them. I ran the cloverleaf pattern three more times, the last at a canter, with Star only missing one lead.

Mr. Baines dropped off real barrels on Tuesday, and Star took to the pattern with no problem. He got better the next afternoon and the next. He wanted to please, and all I had to do was show him what I wanted. I started to believe that Eager Star could actually beat Summer's horse. In between practices with Star, I worked with Towaco, who was getting so gentle Lizzy could have ridden him.

Meanwhile Lizzy and Hawk planned my Friday night sleepover. I wished we hadn't made it the night before the big race. It would seem weird having Summer, the competition, under our roof. But I wanted the party to be a success almost as much as I wanted Star to be a success.

I kept expecting Grant to come by and work with his horse. Twice at school I'd even gotten up courage to ask him, but he made excuses.

Then Thursday evening, as I was unsaddling Star after a good workout—decent time through the cloverleaf with no missed leads—Grant and his dad showed up.

"I'll saddle him again if you want to ride," I said.

Mr. Baines glared at Grant. "Didn't you call her like I told you to?"

Grant dug his hands in his pockets.

Mr. Baines sighed. "I thought my son was down here riding every night. And now he tells me he hasn't made a single practice, and the race is two days away! I'm sure Summer Spidell hasn't waited for the last minute!" He turned to me. "So, have you worked your magic on Bad Boy?"

"I think you'll be pleased with him." I stroked Star's neck.

"I'll be pleased if he beats the pants off Spider." He wheeled on Grant. "And you'll practice tomorrow as long as it takes! Got it?"

"Fine."

"Fine?" Grant's dad mimicked the word. "We'll see how *fine* it is." He turned back to me. "Winnie, okay with you if Grant does a dry run with barrels tomorrow? I'll come by after work and time him myself."

"Sure."

Grant and his dad stared at each other, neither one blinking. The hairs on my arm stood up. Star sidestepped, something he hadn't done in a couple of days. I knew he was picking up on the tension between Grant and his dad. He didn't like it any more than I did.

Finally, Mr. Baines left without another word. The car door slammed and tires squealed.

Grant moved closer to Star and me. "Tell me the truth, Winnie. What are my chances of winning with this horse?" He looked older in the dimly lit barn, with circles under his eyes nobody our age should have. It was hard to believe he was the same herd-leader Grant from AMS.

"Eager Star has really come a long way, Grant. He's a wonderful horse."

"Can we win?" he asked, his voice hard, too loud.

"I don't know," I admitted. "But Star's improved so much in just a week, your dad can't help but be pleased."

Grant let out a bitter laugh that made my skin crawl. "Poor Winnie. You don't know my dad."

could hardly concentrate at school Friday. I was facing the biggest weekend of my life. If my party was a success and Grant won on Saturday, everything would change for me.

All morning I tried to catch Grant alone to talk about the race. As I headed in early to Pat's class, I heard him talking to her.

"Can't you rethink the A−? I could do extra credit to bring it up." Grant sounded desperate.

He's complaining about an A− on his success paper?

I'd felt pretty good about my C+. I'd misspelled a bunch of words and used run-on sentences. But Pat wrote that she loved the part about steps being more important than finish lines. That made me feel pretty good. *I* didn't complain.

"Sweetheart," Pat said, "you can do extra whatever until the cows come home, no offense. But I'm done with these papers."

I backed away until I saw other kids go in. I'd have to wait to talk to Grant about Star. He had other things on his mind.

That afternoon the help-line e-mails took longer than usual. When I finished, I headed straight for the barn. Eager Star whinnied. I sensed tension before I saw what was wrong. At the end of the stallway, Grant Baines had Star halfway into the cross-ties.

"Grant, don't!" I yelled.

"Where's the other strap?" He sounded frustrated. He and Star were both sweating.

"Your horse broke it!" I snapped. I grabbed the leadrope from him and dropped it. "Star doesn't need cross-ties!"

"Get on with it! Dad will be here soon!"

Star stepped backward. "Not so loud," I said. "Star will think you're scolding him."

Grant patted his horse on the forehead so hard it echoed.

"Don't pat him like that. Think like a horse. They scratch with their teeth or rub noses. Pats are more like kicks."

Grant flung the blanket and saddle up onto Star's back.

"Careful! Not so rough. And you're cinching him too tight."

This was not going well at all. *God, please . . .* but I didn't know what to pray. What I wanted was for Grant to get out of my way and quit making Star nervous.

"I'll bridle him," Grant said, studying the lighter bit. He grabbed Star's ear, then thrust the bit at him. Star jerked his head up. Before I could stop him, Grant slapped his horse on the cheek.

"Quit it!" I cried, jerking the bridle out of Grant's hands. "You can't punish Star because you don't know how to put on a bridle!" My heart pounded. *God? Take my anger . . . again! Please!*

"Sorry," I muttered. But I wasn't about to give him back the bridle. I scratched Star's jaw until he calmed down enough for me to slip on the bridle.

I held Eager Star for Grant to mount. "Good,

Star." Grant stuck his left boot into the stirrup and grabbed the saddle horn. "Don't tighten the reins!" I warned.

But he tugged the reins as he swung, off balance, into the saddle. "Whoa! What's wrong with you?" he shouted.

"Your toe dug into his side when you mounted, Grant! *That's* what's wrong with him."

Things went from bad to worse as Grant rode Star around the paddock. His form was good. He knew how to ride. But he punished Star for every little thing, kicking him when he missed the cue to lope, yanking the reins when he didn't stop fast enough, flicking him with the reins for wrong leads.

"Whazzup? Squawk!" Hawk stood at the fence, Peter Lory on her shoulder.

A knot tightened in my stomach, remembering the party that would soon be happening in my very own house. I hoped Hawk and Lizzy had done everything.

"We are all set inside!" Hawk glanced to the pasture. "How is it here?"

I joined her at the fence. "Grant's impossible, Hawk!"

"Is he so bad?" she asked.

I peeked around to see Grant heading for the barrels at an uneven canter. "Yes!"

"Too bad," Hawk said, "because his dad just drove up."

Mr. Baines walked up and nodded to Hawk. "You're Bob Hawkins's daughter, right?"

Hawk shook his hand.

"So how's my horse?"

He obviously hadn't looked out in the pasture, where Grant fought with Eager Star, trying to make him get the right lead.

"He's been doing great!" I said. *Until your son got here.*

"How's his time?" He gazed out at the pasture. "Grant! You ready?"

We joined Grant at the starting line. Star couldn't stand still.

"Think you remember how to do this?" Mr. Baines asked.

"I remember." Grant's breathing came heavy as he struggled with Star.

"Take the course as fast as you can. On your mark . . ."

Star wouldn't stay on his mark. Grant had to circle him again.

"Get set! Go!"

Eager Star lunged forward, galloping from a standstill. But he broke back to a trot as they neared the first barrel.

"What's he doing?" Mr. Baines barked.

I knew Grant was about to kick his horse. Star knew it too. He lowered his head, arched his back.

"Grant! Don't!" I could see Star gather his muscles to buck. The horse wasn't going to change his mind. His nose almost reached the dirt. "Grant, get your seat away from the saddle! Clamp your knees!" I was running toward them, with Grant's dad shouting behind me.

Grant ignored me and rode the saddle. Star uncurled into a giant buck that sent Grant flying over Star's head. He landed in the grass, looking like he was sitting on an invisible saddle.

"You okay?" I squatted down and took his arm, but he yanked it away.

Grant's dad ran up. Concern changed to disgust. "I must have been crazy to think you could beat Summer! I'll call Spider and tell him he wins. No contest." He turned and started off.

"Wait!" I shouted. "It's not fair! Let me show you what your horse can do! Please, Mr. Baines!" Not waiting for an answer, I swung into the saddle without using the stirrup. "Good boy, Star," I murmured.

Grant got to his feet and backed away, bumping into his dad.

I put the humans out of my mind and reached down to scratch Star's shoulder. "Show them what a great horse you really are!"

Eager Star's hooves pawed the starting line.

"On your mark! Get set! Go!" I shouted, giving Star the cue, squeezing with my legs and leaning forward.

Star exploded in a gallop and reined left to the first barrel, leaning into it and circling close, coming out at a gallop to the second barrel. We edged too close and bumped, but the barrel didn't fall over. No penalty. Star changed leads on cue and headed for the top of the cloverleaf, the third barrel. I heard Hawk cheering.

"You're doing great!" I told Star. And he was.

We circled the last barrel a bit wide, but Star leaned in at such a slant I could have touched the ground with my hand. We raced the homestretch, the wind tearing at my face so hard I couldn't see. The finish line streaked beneath us as we slid to a cattle pony stop.

"Good, Eager Star," I whispered.

Hawk ran up and stroked Star's neck. "You did it!" Peter Lory flapped his wings from his perch on Hawk's shoulder. *"Squawk! Did it!"*

Mr. Baines came running up and slapped my knee. "That was amazing! I wish I'd had the clock running. That horse was fast enough to give Spider the race of his life!"

My head felt light. I glanced at Grant. He should have been so proud of his horse.

"Nice ride," he muttered with no enthusiasm.

His dad wheeled around as if he'd forgotten Grant was there. "Nice ride? Is that all you can say? Not only did she stay on the horse, she raced him! I want you to ride like that!"

He turned back to me. "How 'bout it, Winnie? Can you turn my boy into a winner by tomorrow noon?"

"I don't know." It was too dark to ride any more tonight.

Mr. Baines must have read my thoughts. "You make Grant win that race tomorrow, and I'll double your money!"

Double my money? Two months' fee for a week's work? Dad wouldn't believe it! Besides, I wanted to beat Summer almost as bad as he wanted to beat Spider Spidell.

"Deal!" I turned to Grant. "First thing tomorrow—"

But Grant wasn't there. He'd disappeared.

Grant better show at dawn tomorrow!" I told Hawk after Mr. Baines left. "We're out of time, Hawk! I wish *I* could ride Star myself."

Hawk grabbed my shoulders and stared into my eyes. "Focus! Your party, remember?"

My party! "I have to change and—"

"Hey! Is Summer out here?" Sal walked into the barn timidly as if she thought it might cave in. Even in jeans, she looked as out of place in a barn as Hawk's fancy bird.

"Hey, Sal!" I couldn't think of a single thing to say to her.

"Lizzy said Summer hasn't shown yet, but that I could check out here." Sal scratched her arm as if something had bitten her.

"Summer is not here yet," Hawk said.

"Who else is coming?" Sal asked.

Hawk answered for me. "Just you and Summer. Let's go back to the house."

Sal tiptoed out. "What's with the stuff in the yard?"

"Pizza!" Lizzy yelled from the house.

Sal picked up the pace. "I'm starved!"

Inside, I looked around our living room through Sal's eyes. Pale green walls badly in need of paint, no pictures, a gold shag carpet worn flat by the door and the television, Dad's reading chair covered with newspapers, and a couch that never should have left Goodwill. But the musty smell was disguised by the scent of fresh-baked bread and mozzarella cheese.

"Where should I put my pack?" Sal asked. She didn't seem to trust any place she'd seen so far.

I led her to the bedroom, snatching up clothes off my half of the room. Lizzy's half looked perfect. "Throw your stuff over there."

Sal plopped her pack on Lizzy's bed and herself next to it. "Small room, but at least you've got the extra bed for company."

"Lizzy's company. That's her bed, but she and Hawk will sleep on the floor with me tonight. You and Summer can have the beds."

"You share a room?" Sal glanced at the walls.

My half was covered with horse pictures torn from magazines.

I showed Sal where to wash up, explaining that the hot faucet is really the cold. "And the door doesn't lock. You can hang a washcloth over the outside knob so people know somebody's in there."

The phone rang.

"Maybe it's Summer!" Sal almost knocked me down on her way out of the room.

Lizzy answered, then put her hand over the mouthpiece. "Winnie! For you!"

"Is it Summer?" Sal asked.

I dried my hands and picked up the phone. "Hello?"

"Winnie?" It *was* Summer. "I'm not going to be able to spend the night at your house."

"Why not?" I asked.

"Why not what?" Sal asked, crowding in to hear.

"Mother doesn't feel comfortable having me stay there without another mother to chaperone," Summer answered. "You understand."

I understood. Like it was my fault my mother was dead? I rubbed the scar on my elbow. The one I'd gotten in the car accident that had killed my mother. I didn't think there were any new ways left for me to miss my mother, but Summer had found one.

Sal kept trying to press her ear to the receiver.

Summer was still talking. "Dad doesn't really know Odd-Job Willis that well. You know how it is."

I knew how it was.

"Summer?" Sal shouted toward the receiver.

I handed Sal the phone and walked over to Lizzy and Hawk, who looked at me as if I were an old mare just assigned to the glue factory.

"Why didn't you call me?" Sal whined into the receiver. "I know!" She turned her back to us, listened silently for a full minute, then whispered, "Okay!" and hung up.

"Let's eat!" Lizzy produced the most beautiful pizza, oozing with cheese and pepperoni and sausage. We sat at the table and held out our plates.

Dad strolled in, still wearing the one-piece work suit that makes me think of astronauts. "Smells great, Lizzy!"

I introduced him to Sal. "Dad, aren't you going to that business luncheon tomorrow?" I glanced at Sal, but she just bit into her pizza.

Lizzy looked like she wanted to stop her and

bless the pizza first. Quickly she said, "Thanks for this food, God! Amen!"

Sal gave Lizzy a sideways glance as if my sister had just spoken to little green men.

Uncrumpling a list from his pocket, Dad dialed the phone. "Just pretend I'm not here," he told us. He stiffened when he said into the receiver, "Hello there! How are you?" Silence. "Well, I hope it's a fine dinner! The reason I'm calling is that you've been selected to receive—" he frowned at the phone—"hello?"

Lizzy served seconds as Dad dialed another number. "Hello there! How are you? Could I have just three minutes of your time that could change the rest of your life?" Silence.

"I know that voice!" Sal whispered. "Cell phones! He called *our* house at dinner!"

"Oh, dinner won't cool in three short—" Dad hung up and sighed.

Lizzy's pizza stuck in my throat. "Dad, could you hold off until we finish eating?"

"What?" Dad narrowed his eyes at me, then glanced at Sal. "Oh . . . sure. No problem."

I sighed and finished my pizza. Lizzy did most of the talking, with Hawk chiming in now and then.

The minute Sal finished her fourth piece of pizza, she stood up. "Delicious, Lizzy! My brother was right about you." She smiled at me. "I had a nice time, Winnie. Thanks for asking me."

"Had?" I asked, feeling tears swell in the back of my head and press against my eyeballs.

"I'm sorry." Sal wiped her mouth with the thin napkin. "I have to leave. I've . . . had a change of plans."

"You can't!" Lizzy cried. "I made brownies!"

"They smell great! Can I take one with? Two?"

I knew the second one was for Summer. If I could have slipped a dozen laxatives into those brownies, I would have.

Sal scooped the brownies into her napkin. Then she dashed into my room as if rescuing her backpack from a blazing fire.

"Victoria," she called, backing toward the front door. Did she think we'd jump her the minute her back was turned? "See you at school? You too, Winnie?" Sal stumbled, reached behind her for the screen door, and got away.

I was an idiot to think I could be part of their herd! Hawk's head was bowed so I couldn't see her face. "You have a change of plans too, Hawk?"

Hawk lifted her chin. Peter zoomed to the fridge. *"Squawk! Change of plans! Change of plans!"*

Lizzy chuckled. Hawk grinned. It was just what we needed to break the tension. The fight went out of me.

The rest of the night we just hung out. We visited the horses. Hawk taught Lizzy and me about the markings Native American warriors used to paint on their warhorses.

I fell asleep on the floor next to Lizzy's whistling snore, with the sound of a whippoorwill so close it could have been in the room with us.

In my dream, someone was knocking. I woke up to the *tat, tat, tat* of woodpeckers and Peter perched on the windowsill. I was in mid-yawn when I came to my senses. *Saturday! The barrel race is today!*

I wanted to ride, needed to ride. It took two minutes for me to wake Hawk, get dressed, and tiptoe out.

We rode into the sunrise, with Hawk naming

every bird by its song: "Flutest wren, oriole, purple martin."

Towaco behaved perfectly for Hawk. All my hard work was paying off.

We'd turned around on a country road and skirted back through the sleeping town when I heard my name called.

"Winnie!" Mr. Baines drove up beside me. "I've been looking all over for you! Lizzy said you were riding."

I flashed back to the day I'd lost Towaco. "Is something wrong?"

"Something's *right!*" He looked like he'd already won the race. "I want *you* to race Grant's horse!"

"You do?"

"Spidell admitted the race determines which of us got the better horse—nothing to do with the rider. Besides, I could tell he thinks I'm making a big mistake putting you in." He chuckled. "We'll show him!"

I'm riding Eager Star in the barrel race!

Hawk rode Towaco closer. "Winnie, this is what you wanted! I'll ride Towaco home and bring him back in time to watch you race!"

"Thanks, Hawk!" Catman would be there.

And Barker and Lizzy. I'd have my own cheering section. "What's Grant say?" I asked Mr. Baines.

He revved his engine. Nickers reared a couple of inches. "Who knows? He left the house before I got up. I haven't seen him. Don't worry about Grant. What he wants is a win—any way he can get it. And you're it!"

I hoped he was right. I couldn't imagine not wanting to ride my own horse. But his dad knew Grant better than I did.

On the ride home I pictured myself on Star, crossing the finishing line, flashbulbs popping, people cheering . . . Summer whining.

I turned Nickers out and was running to the house to tell Lizzy the good news when I stopped cold. Grant Baines was sitting on the steps eating Lizzy's cold pizza.

I sat beside him. "Grant, I'm sorry."

"Don't be!" he snapped. "I suppose you've told everybody how I got bucked off yesterday." He wouldn't look at me.

"I wouldn't do that."

He got to his feet. "Can we just practice?"

He strode ahead of me to the barn. *Grant's dad doesn't know him as well he thinks he does. On*

*the other hand, Grant couldn't be too upset or he
wouldn't have come over to help me with Star.*

That thought made me feel better, even
though Grant stormed through the barn, banging the lid on the tack box as he pulled out
Star's saddle and bridle.

I felt bad for the way our only practice had
gone. I'd been too tough on him. I thought back
to how many things I'd criticized: *Don't talk loud,
don't pat, don't tighten the reins, don't . . .* It may
not have been punishment, but it sure hadn't
been praise.

Think of people as horses. At church Ralph had
said, "All God's creatures need praise." Watching
Grant slam the saddle down, I wondered if I'd
ever seen anybody who needed praise more
than he did. I wished I could have that practice
back.

Eager Star walked in, and that's when I got an
idea. I didn't need to practice on Grant's horse.
Maybe we'd have time for a do-over after all.
"Grant, why don't you start working out with
your horse? I'd like to try something."

"You're the boss." He didn't sound too happy
about that.

I led Star to the pasture, then handed the

rope to Grant. "Drop the leadrope and walk away."

He did, and his horse stayed while he brought out the tack.

"Well, praise him! He stood still for you."

"I don't know how to praise him!" He said it like I'd asked him to slow dance with me.

"Good boy, Star!" I nodded for Grant to say it.

"Good boy, Star," he said, with one-tenth my enthusiasm.

"That wasn't so bad!"

I made him praise Star five times as we tacked up. By the fifth time, he sounded like he meant it. "He's not a bad-looking horse, is he?" He reached up to pet the bay, but Star jerked his head back, remembering the slap.

"Tell *him*," I urged.

Grant almost grinned. "You're kind of handsome." This time the bay stood still and let himself be scratched.

"You're good with him," I said. "Star likes you."

"You think?" He scratched Star's withers. "You like that, don't you?" I had a feeling he'd never talked to a horse before, except to scold him.

Grant's mount didn't go much better than the

night before, but he kept his cool and didn't raise his voice.

"You two are doing fine!" I called as he settled in the saddle. Star had the jitters, and I thought about taking over. I had the race to worry about. But instead, I taught Grant a calm-down cue that had worked for me with the bay. "When Star tenses up like that, lift one rein. Pull back, but not too much. Good job, Grant!"

As soon as I said it, Grant seemed to relax too.

"Now, when Star drops his head to get out of the pressure, relax your rein."

Almost on command, Star dropped his head. Grant released the rein at exactly the right moment. Star calmed down instantly.

"Way to go, Grant! Praise Star, and do it again whenever you feel him tense."

"If you say so." Grant didn't sound convinced, but he repeated the cue a dozen times in the next hour until Star stopped fighting him. "Good boy, Star!" He reached down and scratched his horse's neck.

Lizzy brought out granola bars, which we scarfed down so we could get back to Star.

We worked our way over to the barrels. Still

mounted, Grant walked Star through the pattern, then trotted, making wide loops. It was hard to believe that this horse and rider were the same ones who'd struggled against each other less than 24 hours ago. Grant praised Star at every turn, and Star obeyed every cue. They took the pattern in a canter. Then Grant galloped Star through the whole thing.

"You two are great!" I screamed as they crossed the finish line, Star not even sweating.

Grant leaned forward to stroke his horse. "Good boy, Eager Star!" It was the first time he'd called his horse that.

Thank you, God! I felt full of praise for the whole world. No way could Star and I lose after this!

"My turn," I said, taking the reins, expecting him to dismount. He'd had his own victory in a way really. Now it was my time.

Grant frowned. "I don't think so, Winnie."

I checked my watch. Spidells would be arriving any minute. "Why not?"

Grant looked puzzled. "Too close to race time. Star and I have to get ready. We could keep him here over the weekend maybe. You could ride him tomorrow?"

I stared up at him, my legs feeling like limp carrots. "What about the race?"

"I know. I have to change boots. Dad would flip if I didn't wear spurs. But don't worry. I won't use them or the whip." He smiled down at me. He wasn't fighting me for the ride. He wasn't trying to get his position back for the race.

"Grant?" My voice cracked, hoarser than normal. "Did you see your dad this morning? Did he . . . talk to you?"

He shook his head. "I guess I avoided him." He stared out to the road, where cars were pulling in. Spidells' trailer stopped in front of the house. "There's Dad now! Winnie, I don't want to let him down." He reached back and scratched his horse's rump. "Star and I won't let him down."

I watched him walk Eager Star to the barn. I ran through all our morning conversations. I'd thought he was helping *me!* He thought I was helping him. He'd figured our training was for the race *he* was running. How could I have been so wrong? Grant had no idea his dad had replaced him!

Chapter 14

I ran so fast that I reached Mr. Baines as he was getting out of his car. "Winnie! There's my—!"

"You didn't tell him! Grant doesn't know I'm riding! *I* can't tell him. You have to!"

"Easy there." He waved to Spidells, who were unloading their horse. "Don't get so worked up. Just get on that horse and win!"

"But you have to—!"

"Spider!" Mr. Baines turned his back on me and joined the Spidells and Pat Haven. He was done with me. "Pat, you come to see me win?"

Mr. Spidell wore a cowboy hat and a blue, fringed shirt that matched Summer's. "Pat, will you tell this loser not to count his chickens before they hatch?"

"No offense!" Pat added, dragging both men, who looked four times her size, by their arms out to the pasture.

Summer followed them, leading her horse, a good-looking chestnut mare. "I hate Western gear . . . ," she whined. I couldn't make out the rest of the complaint.

I can't stand here and do nothing.

Grant and Star were still in the barn. Catman and Barker had arrived with Pat and were walking out to the pasture with Lizzy and Hawk, who'd ridden over on Towaco. I saw Sal join Summer as she walked her horse over the cloverleaf course.

I had to get ready. I ran into the house and bumped into Dad in the hallway. "Sorry." My stomach burned, and I felt tears swimming in my eyes.

"How do I look?" Dad straightened his black tie. The suit looked new, but baggy.

I managed to smile. "Great, Dad."

"Really? Can't believe I used to wear these things all the time." He examined himself in the mirror. "Guess I've lost weight since . . . since I wore this."

My mind shot me a photo—Lizzy crying,

sitting cross-legged on the floor in front of Mom's closed casket. And Dad leaning over her—Dad, dressed in *this* suit, his funeral suit.

Dad sighed. "I really don't want to go to this Ashland business luncheon. But you're right. I need to make a good impression."

Good impression. It was the reason I'd tried so hard to break into Summer's group, the reason I wanted to ride Star and win. But who was I trying to impress? Summer? Not exactly my first choice for best friend. Mr. Baines? I had a feeling he was impossible to impress. Dad? Dad was struggling to impress his own herd.

My mind flashed a picture of Granny Barker staring out at the stars and fireflies. *"Jesus cares more about the steps than the finish line. Can't nobody impress God,"* she had said.

A calm washed over me. *God, help me take the right step.*

"Winnie, shouldn't you get ready for the race?" Dad asked.

I jumped up and planted a kiss on his cheek. "I'm ready! And you better change out of that thing and into your astronaut suit and get to the pasture!"

"But the luncheon? Those businessmen?"

"They'll just have to eat without Odd-Job Willis. You have a barrel race to watch!" I grinned at my dad, and something happened between us. I knew he felt it too. A kind of relaxing, like Star got from Grant when he'd loosened that rein and said, "Good boy, Star."

Dad hurried off to change, and I tore out to the barn and caught Grant hugging Eager Star.

"Grant, wait here with Star until Summer races. I'll come get you when it's Star's turn."

I waved to my cheering section—Catman, Barker, Hawk, and Lizzy. They were lined up on one side of the pasture, opposite Sal, Summer, Mrs. Spidell, and a photographer.

Hawk ran out to me. "Are you ready?"

"I'm not riding, Hawk," I whispered, glancing toward the barrels, where Mr. Baines and Mr. Spidell were yelling at each other.

"But Mr. Baines said—!" Hawk began.

"I can't do it to Grant, Hawk. He needs to do this. And his dad doesn't know yet, so keep it quiet. Tell Catman and everybody to cheer Grant like they've never cheered before."

Hawk gave my arm a tiny punch. "Good for you, Winnie." Then she ran back to my friends.

The two dads were still arguing as I passed by the barrels.

"I said *I* would time the trials!" Mr. Spidell yelled.

Mr. Baines leaned in until their noses touched. "I don't think so! *I'm* timing!"

"Gents! Stop being so bullheaded! No offense! When are you kids gonna grow up?" Pat shouted. "I'll settle this. Jack?"

All eyes turned toward my dad, who was strolling across the pasture as if the weight of the world had been lifted from his shoulders.

"Jack, you're our official timer!" Pat announced, leaving no room for further argument.

Mr. Spidell explained the rules to Dad. "Don't start the clock until they cross the starting line. They can touch or even move any barrel. But if one gets knocked over, add a five-second penalty. Got it?" Sunlight lit the top of Mr. Spidell's head, and the dark tufts of his remaining hair stuck out like feathers.

"Summer can go first," I said.

Mr. Baines scowled, but the Spidells jumped at the chance. Summer waved to Sal. "Wish me luck!" She backed behind the starting line to give herself a run at it.

Mr. Baines frowned at my old jeans and T-shirt, then glanced around the pasture. "Where's Bad Boy?"

"Grant's got him in the barn," I answered.

Dad raised his hand. "On your mark! Get set! Go!" Down came his hand.

Summer exploded over the starting line, the mare breaking into a gallop and heading for the right-hand barrel. Summer kicked as they rounded the first barrel and headed for the second. Her dad screamed. Sal cheered. Summer yelled as the chestnut took the second barrel and raced to the third. Again and again she kicked, her spurs glinting sunlight like knife blades. The last turn came wide, and Summer swore. She brought out the quirt, a short, rawhide whip, on the homestretch, flicking it and kicking even after she'd crossed the finish.

"Time!" Mr. Spidell shouted.

Mr. Baines ran over to me. "They got a good time. Do whatever it takes to beat it!"

I trotted to the barn, where Grant was waiting by Star's side. "It's time, Grant."

He nodded, and we led Star out to the pasture, stopping a good ways before the starting line. "Summer made it around fast, didn't she?"

"She did," I admitted. "But don't think about that. Don't even think about the race. Think about Eager Star. He'll race his heart out for you now." I turned toward the crowd gathered near the barrels. "Get ready, Dad!"

"Shouldn't I get on now?" Grant gathered the reins.

I waited until I saw Dad lift his arm.

Star hardly moved for the mount. "Way to stand still, Star!" Grant said.

Mr. Baines was running toward us, shouting something we couldn't make out.

"On your mark!" Dad cried. "Get set! Go!"

Star lunged into a canter.

"What are you doing?" Mr. Baines's face was red and sweaty. "He shouldn't be racing! You should!"

"You're going to miss it!" I ran past him as Star took the first barrel easily, leaning farther in than Summer's horse had, cutting off time by staying close to the barrel. He ran fast, but it felt like slow motion to me as I watched Star's legs reach out and grab earth with every stride. Grant leaned forward, his arms high over the horn, elbows out.

"He's . . . he's doing it!" Mr. Baines caught up with me. "They're really moving! Go, Grant! Kick him! Faster! You can do it!"

Spider Spidell stormed up. "What's the big idea telling me this girl was riding. You set me up!"

Grant and Star made the last cloverleaf turn and came around for the homestretch.

"Bring out the whip!" Mr. Baines shouted. "You can win! The spurs, Grant! Use the spurs!"

In that instant I knew Grant heard his dad. His stirrups moved out, ready to deliver a spurred kick. He raised his quirt.

"Do it!" Mr. Baines screamed.

Don't! I prayed. Punishing Star would go against everything we'd worked so hard for. Eager Star deserved praise.

Grant's legs eased back. He dropped the whip. As they crossed the finish line, he leaned forward and hugged Star's neck.

By the time they came to a stop, we were all there to cheer for them. Lizzy was crying. Hawk hugged me. Barker and Catman and Pat stroked Star and congratulated Grant.

Dad announced, "Grant did it in more time

than Summer did. Does that mean Summer won?"

"You bet it does, Willis!" shouted Spider Spidell. "Right, Baines?"

Lizzy shouted, "Yea, Grant!" and did a cartwheel.

Barker and Hawk cheered for Grant.

Catman snapped his fingers, shouting, "Far out, man!"

And Summer and her dad looked at us like we were crazy.

Dad came over and whispered, "Winnie, do you and your friends know that having the most time means you lost?"

I put my arm around him, not remembering the last time I'd done that. "We know, Dad." I'd lost half of my fee, money we needed. But it felt okay, worth every penny.

Grant's dad pushed his way through the cheering crowd and stood at Star's shoulder. "All you had to do was use that whip and your spurs! Instead, you're the loser."

"Only at the finish line," I said, grinning at Grant. "They won every other step."

Mr. Baines shook his head and left.

Lizzy and Dad invited everybody in for brownies. Grant and I cooled down Star, then joined the others inside. We sat around the kitchen table, laughing, going over the race, talking about school, about everything, about nothing.

One by one they left. Finally, Grant and I went out to the barn. He'd decided to leave Star overnight and pick him up in the morning.

"Winnie, want to go for a ride?"

He didn't have to ask twice. We both rode bareback, letting our horses walk side by side under the green, lacy leaves of the willow trees down to the pond. I stole glances at Grant, who seemed more content than I'd ever seen him. Maybe he was seeing it too—that it wasn't so bad not to come in first. I'd started seventh grade wanting to be the most famous horse gentler in the world. Maybe for now I'd be content with the steps along the way, helping each horse, each person, as if only that mattered and not what people thought about it.

A flock of geese flew over in a crooked *V,* honking their own praise as the sun slipped lower in the sky. *Way to go, God! Good job!*

"Did you say something, Winnie?" Grant asked, reaching down to scratch Star.

"Good job," I said.

He smiled and turned back around. The first star of the evening poked through the still-light sky and winked at us, an eager star. It was a praise ride I'd never forget. And for a instant, in the breeze, in the gentle snorts of the horses breathing in time to the steady, padded thud of their hooves, I thought I heard it—God's whispering praise. *Way to go, Winnie! Good job!*

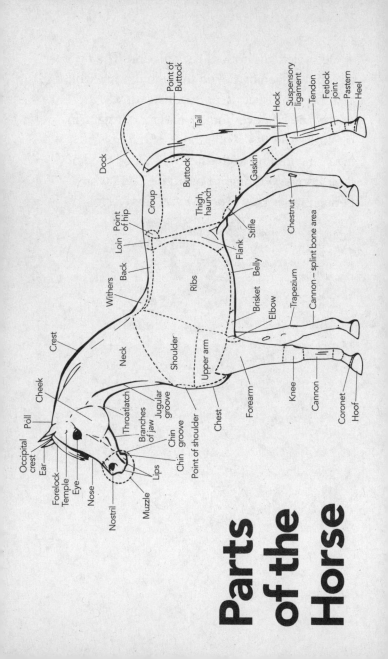

Parts of the Horse

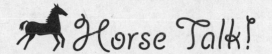# Horse Talk!

Horses communicate with one another . . . and with us, if we learn to read their cues. Here are some of the main ways a horse talks:

Whinny—A loud, long horse call that can be heard from a half mile away. Horses often whinny back and forth.
Possible translations: *Is that you over there? Hello! I'm over here! See me? I heard you! What's going on?*

Neigh—To most horse people, a neigh is the same as a whinny. Some people call any vocalization from a horse a neigh.

Nicker—The friendliest horse greeting in the world. A nicker is a low sound made in the throat, sometimes rumbling. Horses use it as a warm greeting for another horse or a trusted person. A horse owner might hear a nicker at feeding time.
Possible translations: *Welcome back! Good to see you. I missed you. Hey there! Come on over. Got anything good to eat?*

Snort—This sounds like your snort, only much louder and more fluttering. It's a hard exhale, with the air being forced out through the nostrils.
Possible translations: Look out! Something's wrong out there! Yikes! What's that?

Blow—Usually one huge exhale, like a snort, but in a large burst of wind.
Possible translations: What's going on? Things aren't so bad. Such is life.

Squeal—This high-pitched cry that sounds a bit like a scream can be heard a hundred yards away.
Possible translations: Don't you dare! Stop it! I'm warning you! I've had it—I mean it! That hurts!

Grunts, groans, sighs, sniffs—Horses make a variety of sounds. Some grunts and groans mean nothing more than boredom. Others are natural outgrowths of exercise.

Horses also communicate without making a sound. You'll need to observe each horse and tune in to the individual translations, but here are some possible versions of nonverbal horse talk:

EARS
Flat back ears—When a horse pins back its ears, pay attention and beware! If the ears go back slightly, the

horse may just be irritated. The closer the ears are pressed back to the skull, the angrier the horse.

Possible translations: I don't like that buzzing fly. You're making me mad! I'm warning you! You try that, and I'll make you wish you hadn't!

Pricked forward, stiff ears—Ears stiffly forward usually mean a horse is on the alert. Something ahead has captured its attention.

Possible translations: What's that? Did you hear that? I want to know what that is! Forward ears may also say, I'm cool and proud of it!

Relaxed, loosely forward ears—When a horse is content, listening to sounds all around, ears relax, tilting loosely forward.

Possible translations: It's a fine day, not too bad at all. Nothin' new out here.

Uneven ears—When a horse swivels one ear up and one ear back, it's just paying attention to the surroundings.

Possible translations: Sigh. So, anything interesting going on yet?

Stiff, twitching ears—If a horse twitches stiff ears, flicking them fast (in combination with overall body tension), be on guard! This horse may be terrified and ready to bolt.

Possible translations: Yikes! I'm outta here! Run for the hills!

Airplane ears—Ears lopped to the sides usually means the horse is bored or tired.
Possible translations: Nothing ever happens around here. So, what's next already? Bor-ing.

Droopy ears—When a horse's ears sag and droop to the sides, it may just be sleepy, or it might be in pain.
Possible translations: Yawn . . . I am so sleepy. I could sure use some shut-eye. I don't feel so good. It really hurts.

TAIL

Tail switches hard and fast—An intensely angry horse will switch its tail hard enough to hurt anyone foolhardy enough to stand within striking distance. The tail flies side to side and maybe up and down as well.
Possible translations: I've had it, I tell you! Enough is enough! Stand back and get out of my way!

Tail held high—A horse who holds its tail high may be proud to be a horse!
Possible translations: Get a load of me! Hey! Look how gorgeous I am! I'm so amazing that I just may hightail it out of here!

Clamped-down tail—Fear can make a horse clamp its tail to its rump.
Possible translations: I don't like this; it's scary. What are they going to do to me? Can't somebody help me?

Pointed tail swat—One sharp, well-aimed swat of the tail could mean something hurts there.

Possible translations: Ouch! That hurts! Got that pesky fly.

OTHER SIGNALS

Pay attention to other body language. Stamping a hoof may mean impatience or eagerness to get going. A rear hoof raised slightly off the ground might be a sign of irritation. The same hoof raised, but relaxed, may signal sleepiness. When a horse is angry, the muscles tense, back stiffens, and the eyes flash, showing extra white of the eyeballs. One anxious horse may balk, standing stone still and stiff legged. Another horse just as anxious may dance sideways or paw the ground. A horse in pain might swing its head backward toward the pain, toss its head, shiver, or try to rub or nibble the sore spot. Sick horses tend to lower their heads and look dull, listless, and unresponsive.

As you attempt to communicate with your horse and understand what he or she is saying, remember that different horses may use the same sound or signal, but mean different things. One horse may flatten her ears in anger, while another horse lays back his ears to listen to a rider. Each horse has his or her own language, and it's up to you to understand.

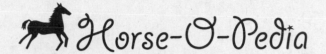

Horse-O-Pedia

American Saddlebred (or American Saddle Horse)—A showy breed of horse with five gaits (walk, trot, canter, and two extras). They are usually high-spirited, often high-strung; mainly seen in horse shows.

Andalusian—A breed of horse originating in Spain, strong and striking in appearance. They have been used in dressage, as parade horses, in the bullring, and even for herding cattle.

Appaloosa—Horse with mottled skin and a pattern of spots, such as a solid white or brown with oblong, dark spots behind the withers. They're usually good all-around horses.

Arabian—Believed to be the oldest breed or one of the oldest. Arabians are thought by many to be the most beautiful of all horses. They are characterized by a small head, large eyes, refined build, silky mane and tail, and often high spirits.

Barb—North African desert horse.

Bay—A horse with a mahogany or deep brown to reddish-brown color and a black mane and tail.

Blind-age—Without revealing age.

Brumby—A bony, Roman-nosed, Australian scrub horse, disagreeable and hard to train.

Buck—To thrust out the back legs, kicking off the ground.

Buckskin—Tan or grayish-yellow-colored horse with black mane and tail.

Cattle-pony stop—Sudden, sliding stop with drastically bent haunches and rear legs; the type of stop a cutting, or cowboy, horse might make to round up cattle.

Chestnut—A horse with a coat colored golden yellow to dark brown, sometimes the color of bays, but with same-color mane and tail.

Cloverleaf—The three-cornered racing pattern followed in many barrel races; so named because the circles around each barrel resemble the three petals on a clover leaf.

Conformation—The overall structure of a horse; the way his parts fit together. Good conformation in a horse means that horse is solidly built, with straight legs and well-proportioned features.

Crop—A small whip sometimes used by riders.

Cross-ties—Two straps coming from opposite walls of the stallway. They hook onto a horse's halter for easier grooming.

Curb—A single-bar bit with a curve in the middle and shanks and a curb chain to provide leverage in a horse's mouth.

D ring—The D-shaped, metal ring on the side of a horse's halter.

English Riding—The style of riding English or Eastern or Saddle Seat, on a flat saddle that's lighter and leaner than a Western saddle. English riding is seen in three-gaited and five-gaited Saddle Horse classes in horse shows. In competition, the rider posts at the trot and wears a formal riding habit.

Gait—Set manner in which a horse moves. Horses have four natural gaits: the walk, the trot or jog, the canter or lope, and the gallop. Other gaits have been learned or are characteristic to certain breeds: pace, amble, slow gait, rack, running walk, etc.

Gelding—An altered male horse.

Hackamore—A bridle with no bit, often used for training Western horses.

Halter—Basic device of straps or rope fitting around a

horse's head and behind the ears. Halters are used to lead or tie up a horse.

Leadrope—A rope with a hook on one end to attach to a horse's halter for leading or tying the horse.

Lipizzaner—Strong, stately horse used in the famous Spanish Riding School of Vienna. Lipizzaners are born black and turn gray or white.

Lunge line (longe line)—A very long lead line or rope, used for exercising a horse from the ground. A hook at one end of the line is attached to the horse's halter, and the horse is encouraged to move in a circle around the handler.

Lusitano—Large, agile, noble breed of horse from Portugal. They're known as the mounts of bullfighters.

Mare—Female horse.

Morgan—A compact, solidly built breed of horse with muscular shoulders. Morgans are usually reliable, trustworthy horses.

Mustang—Originally, a small, hardy Spanish horse turned loose in the wilds. Mustangs still run wild in protected parts of the U.S. They are suspicious of humans, tough, hard to train, but quick and able horses.

Paddock—Fenced area near a stable or barn; smaller

than a pasture. It's often used for training and working horses.

Paint—A spotted horse with Quarter Horse or Thoroughbred bloodlines. The American Paint Horse Association registers only those horses with Paint, Quarter Horse, or Thoroughbred registration papers.

Palomino—Cream-colored or golden horse with a silver or white mane and tail.

Palouse—Native American people who inhabited the Washington–Oregon area. They were hightly skilled in horse training and are credited with developing the Appaloosas.

Pinto—Spotted horse, brown and white or black and white. Refers only to color. The Pinto Horse Association registers any spotted horse or pony.

Przewalski—Perhaps the oldest breed of primitive horse. Also known as the Mongolian Wild Horse, the Przewalski Horse looks primitive, with a large head and a short, broad body.

Quarter Horse—A muscular "cowboy" horse reminiscent of the Old West. The Quarter Horse got its name from the fact that it can outrun other horses over the quarter mile. Quarter Horses are usually easygoing and good-natured.

Quirt—A short-handled rawhide whip sometimes used by riders.

Rear—To suddenly lift both front legs into the air and stand only on the back legs.

Roan—The color of a horse when white hairs mix with the basic coat of black, brown, chestnut, or gray.

Snaffle—A single bar bit, often jointed, or "broken" in the middle, with no shank. Snaffle bits are generally considered less punishing than curbed bits.

Sorrel—Used to describe a horse that's reddish (usually reddish-brown) in color.

Spur—A short metal spike or spiked wheel that straps to the heel of a rider's boots. Spurs are used to urge the horse on faster.

Stallion—An unaltered male horse.

Standardbred—A breed of horse heavier than the Thoroughbred, but similar in type. Standardbreds have a calm temperament and are used in harness racing.

Tack—Horse equipment (saddles, bridles, halters, etc.).

Tennessee Walker—A gaited horse, with a running walk—half walk and half trot. Tennessee Walking Horses are generally steady and reliable, very comfortable to ride.

Thoroughbred—The fastest breed of horse in the world, they are used as racing horses. Thoroughbreds are often high-strung.

Tie short—Tying the rope with little or no slack to prevent movement from the horse.

Trakehner—Strong, dependable, agile horse that can do it all—show, dressage, jump, harness.

Twitch—A device some horsemen use to make a horse go where it doesn't want to go. A rope noose loops around the upper lip. The loop is attached to what looks like a bat, and the bat is twisted, tightening the noose around the horse's muzzle until he gives in.

Western Riding—The style of riding as cowboys of the Old West rode, as ranchers have ridden, with a traditional Western saddle, heavy, deep-seated, with a raised saddle horn. Trail riding and pleasure riding are generally Western; more relaxed than English riding.

Wind sucking—The bad, and often dangerous, habit of some stabled horses to chew on fence or stall wood and suck in air.

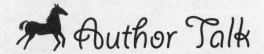 # Author Talk

Dandi Daley Mackall grew up riding horses, taking her first solo bareback ride when she was three. Her best friends were Sugar, a Pinto; Misty, probably a Morgan; and Towaco, an Appaloosa; along with Ash Bill, a Quarter Horse; Rocket, a buckskin; Angel, the colt; Butch, anybody's guess; Lancer and Cindy, American Saddlebreds; and Moby, a white Quarter Horse. Dandi and husband, Joe; daughters, Jen and Katy; and son, Dan (when forced) enjoy riding Cheyenne, their Paint. Dandi has written books for all ages, including Little Blessings books, Degrees of Guilt: *Kyra's Story*, Degrees of Betrayal: *Sierra's Story, Love Rules,* and *Maggie's Story*. Her books (about 400 titles) have sold more than 4 million copies. She writes and rides from rural Ohio.

Visit Dandi at www.dandibooks.com

Winnie
The Horse Gentler

1 WILD THING

2 EAGER STAR

3 BOLD BEAUTY

4 MIDNIGHT MYSTERY

5 UNHAPPY APPY

6 GIFT HORSE

7 FRIENDLY FOAL

8 BUCKSKIN BANDIT

COLLECT ALL EIGHT BOOKS!

CP0015-B

Can't get enough of Winnie? Visit her Web site to read more about Winnie and her friends plus all about their horses.

IT'S ALL ON WINNIETHEHORSEGENTLER.COM

There are so many fun and cool things to do on Winnie's Web site; here are just a few:

⭐ PAT'S PETS

Post your favorite photo of your pet and tell us a fun story about them

⭐ ASK WINNIE

Here's your chance to ask Winnie questions about your horse

⭐ MANE ATTRACTION

Meet Dandi and her horse, Chestnut!

⭐ THE BARNYARD

Here's your chance to share your thoughts with others

⭐ AND MUCH MORE!